August Heat

Illustrations by Inara Cedrins
Design by Emory Mead

Story
Press

P. O. Box 10040
Chicago, Ill. 60610

short
stories
by
richard
dokey

august
HEAT

Acknowledgements

The stories in this book appeared originally in the following magazines: "Birth" in *Epoch;* "Home" and "The Autumn of Henry Simpson" in *South Dakota Review;* "Sanchez," "August Heat," "Port of Call," and "Teacher" in *Southwest Review;* "The Old Maid" in *Michigan Quarterly Review;* "The Dead Man" in *Carolina Quarterly;* "Death Valley" in *Fiction Texas.* The author is grateful to these magazines for permission to reprint.

Library of Congress Catalog Card Number: 81-23346
Copyright © 1982 by Richard Dokey
All Rights Reserved
Printed in the United States of America
A First Edition

Publication of this book was made possible by a generous grant from Carol J. Evans.

Library of Congress Cataloging in Publication Data

Dokey, Richard.
  August heat.

  Contents: Birth—Home—The dead man—[etc.]
  I. Title.
PS 3554.042A95   813'.54   81-23346
ISBN 0-931704-09-X   AACR2
ISBN 0-931704-08-1 (pbk.)

for my daughter Cameron

Without Night, the nature of Man
would receive no income,
so there would be nothing for Day to spend.
—Rumi

Contents

Birth

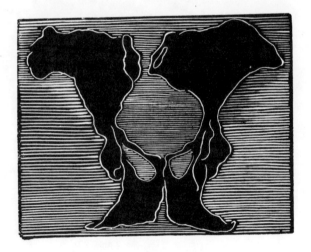

Every day now the ewe was getting bigger and bigger. Billy took it food in the morning, little bunches of hay and carrot tops from the garden. The ewe grabbed the food from Billy's outstretched hand and chewed it in that quick fashion, its long, slender underjaw moving sideways. Billy patted the ewe's head. It felt odd to touch the animal's grey-white coat. The wool lay in corrugated wrinkled ropes and it was like petting the bark of one of the pine trees outside the barn, only smoother, of course. So he only patted the ewe's head and scratched its ears.

Billy sat down in the stall to watch the ewe eat. He looked at the animal's round belly. It was all belly, too much belly, as Tom Watson, the hired hand, would say. Tom Watson knew a lot about sheep and when the time came he would deliver the little lamb. And that's what Billy wanted to see. He was most eager to see that. Always before he would simply walk into one of the pastures when it was time and there would be all those little lambs stumbling and falling about. They would just be there. He had never seen one actually come out but this time he would. The ewe was having trouble. All the other ewes had dropped but this one and so his father and Tom Watson had brought it into the barn to watch and be ready. Billy had that job mainly. Tom Watson would deliver and his father would help but Billy was the watcher. And he was doing that well, better than anyone had realized, for sometimes he sneaked out at night when everybody was asleep, to watch a little. He did not carry a flashlight or even strike a match at those times because someone might have seen and then his mother would have stopped him. So he watched in the dark of the old barn and sometimes there was moonlight in the stall.

And so the ewe just stood there, its big belly almost hiding the thin, wiry legs, and chewed the carrot tops. Always when he came the ewe would be standing. Even at night. He'd come very quietly in the dark to the stall and there would be the ewe, standing and staring out of its little yellow bubble eyes. Now the ewe stood chewing and Billy wondered if ewes could think and what they thought about and could they feel and what they felt about. Tom Watson said they couldn't feel nor think anything. Their minds were like eggshells with the insides gone. Nothing grew or happened in a ewe's head or any other animal head, Tom Watson said. And so Billy looked at the yellow bubble eyes before him and thought that must be a terrible thing, to have feelings and thoughts and know nothing about it.

Just then Billy's mother poked her head over the slats of the stall and said, "Honestly, Billy Harker, you'll be the death of me yet. You know you have chores to do. Where are my fresh eggs?"

"Yes'm," Billy said, jumping up. He knew she wasn't angry. It was just her teasing way. "I was only watching for Dad and Tom Watson."

"You think you're going to watch that little beast into life?" she asked, smiling a bit too much. Billy was Mrs. Harker's only child and she loved him more than she could say and she was always fighting it to not protect him from life.

"No, Mom," he said.

She came around the stall and stood next to him. She put a hand on his shoulder. "It is exciting, isn't it?"

"Oh, yes, Mom," he said.

"Seems to get bigger by the hour."

"It could happen anytime, Mom, just anytime."

She shook him playfully. "You get now and fetch me those

eggs."

"Yes'm."

"I'll watch here a little for you."

Later that morning Billy came back to watch some more. The animal was still standing in the stall, looking vacantly out of its bubble eyes. Billy sat down in the hay. The animal usually turned its head to follow him but this time it stood simply still and quite vacant. The ewe did not blink its eyes and Billy watched how it stood there like one of those clay figures he made from the modeling set he got for Christmas. Then Billy noticed a little trembling pass along the underside of the ewe, a little shiver of movement. He looked at the ewe's eyes and the eyes were bigger and brighter, like they might burst, and the tiny trembling passed along the ewe's belly again. Billy came to his knees and bent forward. Something was happening or getting ready to happen. The ewe simply stood, quite vacant and still. Billy watched but there was nothing else. There were only the barn flies buzzing in the warm air. They landed and crept along the ewe's dirty wool rolls and their green iridescence shone under the dusty shafts of light.

Billy stood up and thought maybe he should fetch Tom Watson but the ewe lifted its head and began that sideways chewing motion with its underjaw. Billy offered the ewe some hay and the animal took it, so Billy only decided to tell Tom Watson what he had seen.

"When can you know?" he asked the hired man.

"Oh, you'll know," Tom Watson said.

"But how, Tom?"

"You'll know," the man said. "And then you come for me an' your pa. We'll get us a lamb. You'll see."

"I want to see it, Tom. I don't want to miss it."

"You'll see it," Tom Watson said. "I won't let it happen unless you're there."

"Does it hurt?"

"Does what hurt?"

"When it happens? Does it hurt the ewe?"

"No," Tom Watson said.

"Does it hurt the lamb?"

"No, it doesn't."

"But why doesn't it?" Billy asked.

"Are you writing a book?" Tom Watson joked.

"But it could hurt, couldn't it, Tom?"

"They're not people, boy. They're dumb animals. They're just animals."

"But don't they cry and bleat?"

"Sure they do."

"Well, that's hurt."

"But they don't know it, boy."

"I remember that time Prince got stepped on by that milk cow. He yelped and yowled and ran around screaming. He didn't eat for three days, Tom."

"I thought we'd have to shoot that ol' dog," the hired man said.

"But he hurt, didn't he?"

"Sure, but he didn't know it. Animals don't have minds or souls, boy. They're animals. They're just animals."

"I know," Billy said.

"All they are is animals." He patted the boy's shoulder. "Now I expect it's time for you to check again, ain't it?"

"Yessir," he said, and bolted toward the barn.

In the late afternoon Billy watched the animal some more. It stood as always, indifferent, placid and unmoving in the darkening stall. Billy sat down and watched for those tiny shivers to run along the animal's flanks but nothing happened. What am I supposed to be looking for? he wondered. Then he fed the ewe some more carrot greens and went into the big house for supper.

It was dark when he came out again. The farm was quiet in the still, warm air. Sometimes one of the cattle made that low moaning sound from the back of its throat and the sound lifted and rolled across the field toward him like a wind swirl. It was quite clear and the stars were very bright and open against the black sky. The moon would not be up for hours. Billy looked at the white stars and wondered about them.

Then he ran toward the barn. It was early yet and he hadn't

gone to bed so it was all right to turn on the lights. He went to the stall and there was a cord with a bulb at the end of it. He turned the switch. A bath of yellow color flooded the stall.

The ewe was standing as always but did not turn its head to look at him. That was just like before and Billy dropped to his knees and stared at the animal's swollen belly. The ewe was shivering. All along its sides there was this shivering. Billy watched carefully. He looked at the ewe's eyes. The eyes had flattened and were withdrawn and distant. That was different, Billy thought. He hadn't seen that yet. Then the animal commenced to shake and its back legs began to tremble. Billy watched and watched. Then the ewe sighed a breathing, porous sigh and began to settle down. Its legs seemed simply to melt and it just went down and over on its side very slowly, like the last half turn on a big rubber ball.

Billy jumped to his feet and ran out of the barn. He ran straight to the bunkhouse. His heart was beating wildly when he slammed open the old screen door. Tom Watson was sitting at a wooden table playing solitaire.

"Tom!" Billy shouted.

Tom Watson rose and grabbed his hat all in one motion. "Go fetch your pa," he said.

Billy raced to the big house and his father was just sitting down to read the paper. "Dad! Dad!" he said. "It's happening! It's happening!"

"All right, Son," Billy's father said.

"Dad!"

"Did you fetch Tom?"

"He's on his way now," and he bolted from the room and ran out into the night air.

Tom Watson was already there when Billy arrived. He was kneeling beside the ewe and his hands were lost inside its body. A two foot iron bar was leaning against the wooden slats of the stall.

"It's the wrong way," Tom Watson said to himself, and just then Billy's father came up.

"What is it, Tom?" he asked.

"Wrong way," Tom Watson said.

Billy's father knelt in the hay beside the hired man and put his hands on the animal's belly.

"Feet are twisted around," Tom Watson said. "I don't know about this one."

Billy's father didn't say anything.

"I'll have to take it by the hind legs," the hired man said.

Tom Watson crept closer and his forearms disappeared into the ewe's thick body. Billy stood beside the animal's head watching. The ewe simply lay on its side. Its yellow bubble eyes still retained that vacant, withdrawn stare, as though they were looking at something inside its head. Billy leaned forward and·he saw two tiny legs slide out of the animal's stomach.

"There," Tom Watson said.

The little legs were very white and the coat was matted and wet. Tom Watson worked some more and the hind quarters appeared, like a knotted, white fist.

"What do you think, Tom?" Billy's father said, holding the ewe's belly.

"She's not helping," Tom Watson said. "No strength. I'll have to pull it out."

Billy stood back a little as Tom Watson moved his hands inside the ewe's stomach. A thin smear of red became visible against the white wool of the lamb and then widened and began to flow into the wet wrinkles of its tiny body.

"I was afraid of that," Tom Watson said.

"You'll just have to pull it, Tom," Billy's father said.

Tom Watson nodded and moved his hands some more. The blood came in a little rush and Billy could see it shining on Tom Watson's arms. It was coloring the yellow hay. Some of it was on the knees of Tom Watson's pants. Billy's father looked at Billy and there was a frown on his face. He was going to say something but changed his mind.

Billy watched and watched.

"I'm just going to have to," Tom Watson said. "No other way."

"It's one of those few times all right," Billy's father said.

Tom Watson took a firm grip on the tiny lamb and leaned his weight back. Slowly the two bodies began to separate.

"I think one of the legs is still twisted," Tom Watson said. He moved his hand around inside. "Damn that blood," he said.

The red stuff shone like liquid soap on Tom Watson's arms. It was all over the hay and on Tom Watson's shirt and pants. Some of it was on Billy's father.

Billy stood back, staring. The ewe rested on its side, its eyes rolled back and empty, and then there was a wet plop and the lamb was out. It was clotted with blood and gore and Billy's father took it in his hands. It tried to lift its tiny head and the tinier legs kicked feebly.

"It's fine," Billy's father said, looking at the ewe.

Tom Watson held his hands away from his body. The hands were red and the blood dripped from them. He tried to wipe them on the hay and small bits and stalks stuck to his skin. The blood leaked out of the ewe's empty stomach.

"What do you think, Tom?" Billy's father said.

Tom Watson just shook his head. Billy's father looked at Billy.

"Go fetch an old towel from the bunkhouse," he said. "For Tom's hands."

Billy backed away.

"Go on now."

Billy turned and ran toward the barn door. But he remembered the box of rags under the work bench. He found an old one and stepped back to the stall. Billy's father was gone. He had taken the lamb out the side door to the trough to clean it. The door was open and Billy could see him.

Tom Watson was standing over the ewe. Billy could see the yellow bubble eyes, still distant and away. The ewe was breathing easily but nothing else moved. There was blood all over the hay and the blood still leaked thinly from the animal's body. It was then that Billy noticed the iron bar Tom Watson was holding.

Tom Watson stepped closer to the ewe and set himself. Billy caught his breath.

Tom Watson raised the heavy bar above his head and then swung it downward. There was a sound like no other Billy had ever heard. The animal's body seemed to jerk upward and blood spurted everywhere. Billy watched, horrified, as Tom Watson raised the iron bar and struck again. This time the sound was wet and Billy thought he would be sick. Tom Watson stood looking down at the dead ewe. He had not even realized that Billy was there.

Blood was on Tom Watson's hands. Blood was all over the ewe and all over the hay. Some was on Tom Watson's boots and some was splattered against the slats of the stall. Billy looked down. Glistening on his shirt, there between the second and third buttons, was a drop of red. It shone in the yellow light like a broken jewel.

Billy turned and ran from the barn. He tore the shirt from his body. He stood under the night, holding the shirt by one sleeve, and started to cry. Then after awhile he stopped crying and he went out behind the house where the fifty gallon incinerator drum was and he buried the shirt under the ashes.

He walked into the house.

"Billy," his mother said, "where's your shirt?"

Billy just walked past her.

"Billy, where's your shirt?"

"Outside," he said.

"Honestly, Billy, some day you'll—"

But Billy ran out of the room and up the stairs.

He went to bed. Inside his head he looked at the dead ewe. He looked at the little lamb. He did not want to see the lamb anymore. He didn't even like the little lamb. He didn't like anything. He tried to go to sleep. He wanted to go to sleep. But his eyes just kept looking at the dark.

Home

He came up from the field and stood at the screen door of the kitchen peering in. She knew he was there. She kept her back to the door and went on with the pie crust, pushing the dough against the edge of the pan with her thumb. She began to hum to herself, trapping the sound between her nose and throat when she exhaled. He put his hands in his pockets and frowned.

She knew he was waiting and what he would do. She went on with the pie, her fingers moving swiftly and surely, turning the pan and working the dough. When he shuffled his feet on the wooden planking, she allowed her eyes to flick upward. She smiled. Presently he kicked at the screen door and because it was loose on its hinges it flapped against the frame. She grinned to herself but her eyes sparkled angrily. How like him that was and how exasperating! She turned.

"Jed Angers," she said.

"I got the fence mended."

She wiped her hands on the apron. "Well, are you going to stand there?" she said. He did not answer. She stepped to the door. "Are you just going to stand there?" He kept his eyes fixed steady on hers. "Well, come in, then," she said. "I can't talk to you through this screen."

She was angry. The heat of it flared in her like a match. He could always touch her like that. He could make her hackles rise like no other person she had ever known. He could touch fire in her and afterward she'd fall down a long stair of remorse and shame to live in the dark cellar of her loneliness, where she would wonder how far away and how close she could be to him all at once.

She walked back to the pie pan and he came over to stand beside her. He was smiling. It was as though the anger warmed him and gave him permission to speak. He stood beside her and watched her hands kneading the dough.

"Smells good in here," he said.

"Well, it ought to," she said. "Been working all morning."

He looked over to the window sill where another pie and three loaves of bread were cooling.

"I can see it," he said. He bent forward. "Sure smells good. You sure can cook, Emily. I always said you were a good cook. Even way back I said that. Remember?"

A tall, dark-haired boy with long arms and large wristbones, who spread the checked tablecloth upon the grass for that first picnic, there by the river. Chicken, salad, chocolate cake—he had eaten like a starving man. She smiled and remembered.

"When can I have a piece?" he asked, laying a hand gently against her spine.

"You know the answer to that," she said.

"Supper's too long to wait. I like pie when it's hot. You know I like it when it's hot."

"The pie's for supper. Do you want to spoil your supper? All these years and you haven't changed a bit. No wonder we always have to remind Billy to do his chores."

It was like an invisible knife and she held the point of it against his flesh. He stiffened and wet his lips. "Billy's all right," he said. "He's a good boy."

"You hate doing chores too, you know you do. I've been after you to fix that screen door."

"I'll fix it," he said.

"And then you go and kick it, playing games."

Now he was truly angry, now he could look at her, his dark, shy eyes could hold hers. She loved and hated those eyes. She was crawling around in that dark cellar. She could feel the shame and guilt muddying about her. She could feel the pain flowing from them both.

"Would you like a piece of pie, Jed?" she asked.

"I don't want a piece," he said. "I'll wait for supper."

"Why don't you have a piece now? It's hot, the way you like it."

"I'll wait," he said. "I'll just wait."

They were silent. They stood helpless in the silence and the wind blew quietly from the fields and over the sweet things set on the window sill. The wind brought the smell of new cut hay and they both sensed it in the silence and understood but it was impossible to speak.

Billy Angers was a dreamer. He had started dreaming when he was seven, that time when his father had beaten him in the barn and Buck, the old, faded sorrel, who was dead now, had kicked and plunged in his stall, kicking out the slats of his stall in his fear and fury. Billy had just gone off by himself, that was all, he had just slept overnight in the fields by himself, and his father had beaten him with the old strap until his bottom bled, all for just going off and sleeping alone in the fields, and the expression on his father's face was like a photograph pasted in his mind—a look of pain and confusion that wasn't even connected to him, Billy, but was working on someplace deep within his own anger. It was like his father wasn't even there, and after that he never struck or was harsh with him again.

There was just a lot of work to do, a lot of things to remember, and that's when Billy dreamed the best. Forking hay in the stalls or washing the barn floor, the smell of dung, dust and dry wood as familiar as his own breath around him, he dreamed of the distant Sierra Nevada, of a cabin there and of fishing for trout, of early, cold mornings when the smoke hung in the air and the pines were all damp shadow except for the tips, which burned in a yellow-green fire. He dreamed of travelling to places and meeting people and with these people he was alive, they drew close to him and wanted him close, and he dreamed of women. He loved them, took them, was swallowed by them, satisfied them and most of all gave them themselves because of his aliveness. And sometimes his mother would catch him dreaming, standing there, the hose in his hand, flooding the stalls, staring at the rafters of the barn. "Get it done, Billy!" she would say, and then she'd smile, and that smile would penetrate to his center and declare the dreamer real, while her finger pointed menacingly at the neglected hose. And that confused him.

He was a tall boy, with a shock of black hair like his father's and his father's long arms and awkward shy grace. They often worked side by side. They seldom talked. They sweated together and worked and when Billy glanced at his father's face, it had a set, resigned look, as though he had been condemned to this by something or somebody. He worked hard and always did a good job at everything but there was this look, and sometimes, stopping to mop his brow or take a drink of water from the canvas bag, he would look up at the blue sky or stare away to the East where the mountains were. When Billy saw this look, he wanted to make one of his dreams suddenly come true. The look made him so distant from his father, yet so close, as though he were looking at him privately from behind a curtain, it was so peculiar and frightening, knowing him like that and yet not knowing him at all.

He thought about it. He thought about it working next to his father in the fields. He thought about it lying in bed before sleep. He thought about it and thought about it. He traced it to that beating in his seventh year. A thousand times he watched Buck kick and rear, trying to break free from his stall. A thousand times he studied his father's face, full of doubt and suffering. A thousand times he felt his own pain and bewilderment, because it had been like simply doing something he had been told, though he was never told in so many words, like hearing a voice in his ear and following it, and his father had beaten him for doing as he was told, and that was confusing and so the dreaming had started. His father never beat him for dreaming.

Across the wide green field came the young man with the

dark hair and large wristbones. He walked with an ambling gait that was peculiarly graceful and yet awkward. It was Jed Angers, who said he loved her, who put his hands on her in the dark under the porch, who smelled always faintly of barns and horses and hay, smells she loved. All her life Emily had worked and she knew she would work as Jed Angers' wife, but in that summer there was the promise of something else, and it rose up from so deep within her that she felt naked when she touched it. How often she thought of those early days, like now in the afternoon, fussing over supper. She smiled when she thought of it and the smile did not belong in the kitchen, with the fresh baked bread and pies, with the roast and cold milk. The smile belonged someplace she didn't understand, outside someplace, maybe in those early years. How proud she was of her work and her ability! There was no one else in the county could set a table as neat, keep a house or sew a quilt as fine. But always she smiled and that's what Jed Angers had liked.

"How come you always smile?" he would ask her, like helping her with the dishes so her mother could rest. "You smile just like your old man."

"Now mind you dry that plate proper, Jed," she would say. "We have plenty of clean towels."

"You always smile," he said, turning the plate carefully, rubbing it carefully.

"Do I?" she said.

"You're a cuss," he said. "You're a mystery."

"I'm not a cuss," she said, pouting deliberately. "Just because you can't figure me out."

"Do you know why you smile all the time?"

"Maybe I'm just happy at catching a big ol' lazy boob farmer like you."

He held her around the waist and put his lips against her hair. "That is kind of exciting, ain't it, Em?"

She stopped moving her hands in the soapy water. She felt the warmth of his words settle inside her. "Yes," she breathed.

"I love you so, Em."

"I love you, Jed."

She turned and he put his arms about her and she floated against him. His kiss sent her away, like to the place the smile went, and she did not know where that was but it was like nothing else she had experienced.

"Em—"

"Don't ask me, Jed."

"I want to ask you, Em. You know how we feel. It's foolish to wait."

"It's not the proper thing, it's not right."

"That don't make any difference, Em. The love between us, that's the only right."

She laid her head against his chest. "Oh, Jed, Jed, don't tempt me. I swear that's the part of you I love so. You don't care. It don't make any difference. There's a whole part of you like that, and it frightens me and yet it thrills me so."

"I want you, Em. We're marrying at the end of the summer. You know there's only so much life. It's foolish to waste it."

She trembled and brushed a hand through her hair, streaking it with soap.

"What is it makes you not care so?" she asked. "Everything you do, you do well, but you don't care about it. Somehow you never care about it."

"You're changing the subject on me," he declared.

"Will you not care about me, Jed?"

"Now you know that's not so, Em, you know it."

In the deepest, truest way she knew. "It bothers me, though."

"Like your smile bothers me."

She looked at him. "I never thought of it together like that," she said.

He took a plate from her and dried it carefully. "A man needs a trade and farming's all I know. It's all Pop knows. I'll farm because it's all I know. What a man does don't make all that much difference, does it? It's just what you have to do. Why should it matter so much? If it matters what a man does, then—"

"What?" she asked.

"I—I don't know," he said. "I was going to say something but then it just left my head and I can't remember it." He set the dish down slowly.

"The look of puzzlement on his face frightened her. She had never seen such a look, like that of a little, lost boy, and she threw her arms around him.

"Em," he said.

"Hush, now."

"Please, Em. I need you so."

"Now hush."

"It's warm out tonight. Let's go for a walk. Let's walk in the fields."

"All right," she said.

They finished the dishes and went outside. The air was soft and warm and the fields smelled of growing. The oak trees stood high and bold and dark and the stars looked as though you could walk among them and scatter them about.

"It's lovely," she said.

"Yes," he said.

"It all makes you feel like there was nothing else in the whole world and there was no one but us."

He led her through the heavy oaks.

"Like everything was free," she said, "and there was no hurt or reason for hurt and no shame."

In the trees there was a place and he spread his jacket and they lay down. Then he lay upon her and all the stars commenced to move like dancing fires. She watched the fires. She wanted it so but was so afraid and the stars burned and it didn't seem to matter, they were so unconcerned and the oaks were so indifferent and the grass and earth were without opinion. There was only life and they were the only life and it was only what they were that gave any meaning at all. In the fear and passion she experienced the surprise of herself, and she smiled.

Later, when the stars drew back and the darkness calmed, she was ashamed.

"Jed?" she asked.

"Yes, Em."

"I feel funny. I feel bad."

"Now, Em." He put his arm around her but she felt no heat and she knew he must be feeling something too.

"We should have waited," she said.

"Don't, Em, don't talk about it."

"We should have waited. I love you. It was the most exciting thing that has ever happened to me, but it frightens me and we should have waited."

"No, Em, don't spoil it. Please don't talk that way."

She felt that self retreating, drawing farther and farther back into a deep, dark place.

"I know it's the same with you. I can feel it from you."

He took his arm from around her and they sat facing the darkness side by side.

"What if I should get pregnant? What if there should be a baby?"

"Em," he whispered.

"What would people think? I'd be so humiliated. To have our baby conceived like that. I couldn't bear it. And what would Mother say? She'd never forgive me."

He said nothing. All the joy had left him. He had never known what it would be like. In those few moments he had lost his shyness, his awkward, clumsy groping at life, and been strong and free.

"Em."

"I want to get married," she said.

He did not say anything.

"Jed? You do care about this, don't you?"

"All right, Em," he said.

And they were married, without ceremony or celebration. It was five years before they had Billy.

The sun was sitting on the edge of the window sill when Jed Angers opened the screen door. Billy followed him in and they went over to the sink to wash up for supper. Emily put on the stew, the lettuce and tomato salad, the bread, butter and milk. She cut big wedges of pie.

"Lord, I'm starved," Jed said. "How about you, Billy?"

"I could eat a horse," said Billy.

"Thank goodness tomorrow is Sunday and we can all be lazy," said Jed.

"Maybe you can get after that screen door, Mr. Lazybones," said Emily, smiling.

"Now you would try to spoil a man's supper," he laughed, but there was an edge to the laugh. "I kinda thought maybe Billy and I'd go fishing tomorrow. What do you say, Billy?"

"Okay," said Billy. "We could do that."

"We'll fetch some worms out of the worm bed tomorrow and get us a mess of catfish. Catfish would taste good for Sunday supper. Pass the milk, Em."

"Wish I could afford to go fishing," said Emily.

Jed filled his glass with milk, swallowed it down and refilled the glass. He looked at his wife and then at his son.

"Why, Em, why don't you come with us? Do you good."

"I have some mending to do. Things got to be done. Somebody has to care."

"Em—"

"Honestly, Jed, that screen door has been banging in the wind for months now."

"Do you have to try to ruin every Sunday for me, Em?"

Billy moved the potatoes and meat on his plate and buttered a piece of bread. The words found a place to rest somewhere in his head but he did not pay attention to them. He began to create pictures, like still paintings, in his mind. There was a cabin, there were the mountains, a naked girl flashed in and away, he stood alone on a busy street watching the people.

"I don't want to ruin your Sunday," Emily said, stabbing at a carrot with her fork. "It's just such a nuisance having that door that way. Why don't you fix it?"

"A man just can't keep postponing his pleasures," Jed muttered. "It's like I always have to ask permission."

A pained expression crossed Emily's face. "What do you mean?" she said.

"I don't know," he said. "I don't want to argue, Em. Can't it wait?"

"It always has to wait," said Emily.

"And I always have to wait for a little relaxation, a little fun. You're always reminding me of what I must do. When the door's fixed, it'll be something else."

Emily reddened and he felt his own face grow warm. He did not know how but some deep chord had been struck between them. He felt it pass back and forth. He felt it open some part of himself he wanted her to know about, but just as soon it closed again.

"I'm sorry, dear," she said. "Would you like some more stew?"

"All right," he said.

"How about some bread and butter? You know I baked it fresh today."

"I'd like that, Em."

"And I've cut the biggest piece of pie for you."

"I love your pie, Em. Listen, I'll get to that door first thing in the morning. I'll do it before we go fishing."

"No, no, now I wouldn't think of it. You need to have fun and go off and do what you want. The door can wait, dear." She smiled broadly. "Catch a big one for me."

"Em —"

"I insist now. I only wish I had your free spirit. All our lives I've loved that in you."

"Me, Em?"

"Your free spirit, your ability not to care. I wish I didn't have to care."

"Oh, Em," he said, "Em." He set the fork down upon the plate. "Don't, Em."

"Billy knows what I mean, don't you, Billy?"

Billy was making pictures with his mind.

"Leave the boy out of it, Em."

"Billy?" she said. "Billy."

"Yes'm," he said.

"You see?" she said.

"He wasn't even listening, Em. He doesn't even know what

we were talking about." He shoved his plate away. "I'm really not too much hungry."

"Jed."

"We'll go fishing in the morning, Son. I wouldn't fix that door now if my life depended on it."

"Jed Angers!" she declared.

He got up from the table, poured himself a cup of coffee and left the kitchen. She sat, hurt, yet peculiarly triumphant. She held her fork tightly in her hand.

"Don't pay any attention to your father, Billy," she said, smiling. "He's not really that way. Don't pay him any attention."

Billy was dreaming about the Sierra Nevada.

The following morning Jed rose early. He got dressed, tiptoed into the kitchen, put on the coffee and then went outside. The sun was just on the horizon, where everything was pink and orange. Above him the grey sky was turning to white. Dark shadows fell away from the barns and trees. Fox, his Irish setter, came over to greet him, his ears back and tail wagging. The air was already beginning to warm.

He got a shovel and empty coffee can from the tackle room and walked over to the horse trough. The ground was always damp between the trough and the fence. There were always plenty of worms. He drove the shovel into the soft earth and turned it over. Four or five worms, their reddish wet bodies gleaming in the early light, wiggled confusedly. He broke the shovelful with his hands and a dozen more appeared. He took his time, dropping the worms one by one into the can and sprinkling them with moist earth. He enjoyed this almost as much as the fishing. From time to time he looked up wonderingly. The sun rose higher and the sky turned blue.

Emily woke immediately when he got up. She could never sleep without him there beside her, but she pretended to sleep. She smiled to herself, feeling him moving about, getting dressed and then making coffee before going outside. In many ways he was so considerate of her and she was ashamed for treating him the way she did. Then she felt a hot desire for him. She opened her eyes, sat up in bed and was going to call to him to return, but she lay back down and pulled the covers to her chin. Better to wait, she thought. Tonight would be better. She let her body grow all warm under the blankets thinking about it, then she sighed, pushed them away and got up to fix breakfast.

She went into the kitchen. The coffee was done. She poured herself a cup and then went to the window. She could see Jed digging over by the horse trough. He looked like a ghost in the early light. Billy must still be in bed. Lazybones, she thought, and padded to his room. The door was closed, of course. She knocked. No answer. She knocked again. "Billy?" she said. "Billy." She turned the knob. "Billy, your father's already up getting the worms. Shouldn't you be helping him?" She opened the door wide and looked in. The room was empty. The bed had not been slept in.

The emotion she felt at that moment was so strong and unnerving. It was like she knew, she understood he could be gone but knowing it frightened her, it terrified her. She rushed into the kitchen. "Jed!" she called. She flung back the screen door and ran across the open ground toward the horse trough. "Jed!" she screamed.

He dropped the worm can and looked up. He sat on his haunches looking at her for a long moment. "Em?" he said.

"Jed! Jed!" she called, "he's gone, Billy's gone!" She ran to him, fell into his arms and burst into tears.

"What? What do you mean?" He held her at arm's length.

"I went to his room. Just now. His bed's not been slept in. He's gone."

He put his arm around her and let his eyes roam about the ranch. He looked off toward the mountains. "Nonsense," he said. "he's just up early messing around somewhere. Billy!" he yelled. The sound bounced off the barns and returned. "Hey, Billy!"

"He's gone, Jed. Oh, I know he's run away, that's what he's done. I know it."

"That's silly," he said, wetting his lips. "Now, why would

he go and do a fool thing like that? Did you look about his room?"

"No," she said, drying her eyes, "I was so frightened. I came right after you."

"All right, now," he said, "let's go to his room."

He kept his arm around her and they went quickly to the house. Once inside, Jed ran to Billy's room and stood there, looking about vacantly. Emily went to the bed, pulled the covers back and lifted the pillow. "There's not even a note." She began to cry again.

"Look in his closet," he said. "Are his clothes all there? Look, woman!"

She fumbled through his things. "His sweater's gone," she said, "and those two blue shirts he liked. I washed them yesterday." She knelt down. "And his suitcase is gone."

"All right, now," he said quietly, half to himself, "all right. You call Sheriff Cutter and tell him to hightail it over here. I'm going to take the pickup and drive down the road a ways. Maybe I can find him."

He raced outside and jumped into the truck. He was gone a half hour when Sheriff Cutter's Jeep met him coming back.

"What the hell's this about Billy, Jed?" Cutter said. He was a round man with a round face. "What'd the boy do?"

"Nothing. He didn't do nothing. Just up and lit out."

The sheriff smiled. "Hell, all boys run away from home one time or another. I did it when I was a kid, didn't you?"

"No," he said.

"Well, we'll find him, don't you fear. He can't have gotten far. We'll have him back by the end of the day. Don't you fear. They always come home sooner or later." And he was gone.

Jed drove back to the house. Emily was waiting for him. He climbed out of the cab and took her hand.

"It's all right," he said.

"What did Cutter say?" she asked.

"They're looking for him. They're all out looking for him. He'll be back by supper. Don't worry."

"I'm frightened, Jed."

"I know," he said, "I know. But he's a good boy. He'll be careful. Just a matter of time. They'll find him."

"Buy why, Jed, why?"

"Just a fool kid stunt. Weren't you ever young once?" he looked up at the sky and then away toward the mountains. "C'mon, I want some coffee."

They went inside and Emily poured the coffee and they sat at the kitchen table. He finished one cup and stood up.

"What are you going to do?" she said.

"Best thing is to stay busy. I think I'll fix that screen door. You ought to find something for yourself."

"All right, Jed," she said.

He fetched his tools, removed the door and took it outside. The screen was loose, and he began to tack it carefully into place, working mechanically.

Inside, Emily watched him from the kitchen window. His shoulders were stooped slightly with age but as strong as ever. She watched him, softening to him, growing warm to him, deep to him. He looked up at the sky. It was almost a look of exultation, of triumph and it confused and troubled her because it touched the excitement she felt over what Billy had done. She looked at him and in that moment she wanted him fiercely and passionately. Across the long, long space she met him with pity and shame and love. He looked away toward the mountains and she smiled.

The Dead Man

They brought Billy Parker in from the field and laid him on the loose hay behind the barn. In the late afternoon the sun was on the other side and it was cool in the shade. There was the smell of water down the rows of corn and he could see the cattle at the watering trough and watch them swish their broomstick tails at the green, iridescent flies.

The men all came and stood around and then some of them squatted and looked for twigs or bits of wood to trace patterns in the brown dust. John Higgins, the owner, knelt beside Billy and offered him a drink of water.

"Mary is calling the doc now, Billy," he said. "You just rest easy."

Billy took the water into his mouth and nodded his head. Against the dirt-colored face his lips seemed painted with red enamel. His eyes looked like shiny marbles.

Then Mary Higgins came out on the front porch of the house and looked across the empty space to where all the men were. She was holding her son's hand tightly.

"What's happening?" Tommy wanted to know.

"It's something with one of the men."

"Why'd you call Doc Mertins? What's wrong?"

She stood watching the men. She wanted her husband to turn around so she could signal him but he was too busy. She didn't want to go over there and she didn't want to send Tommy over there. A little puff of wind touched her neck curls and reminded her of something pleasant.

"What happened?" Tommy said.

"Nothing. An accident. That's all. They happen. You have to expect they'll happen."

"Can I go see?"

"You stay here, young man!"

He had been holding his mother's hand in return but now he relaxed his grip and his arm appeared to dangle from her firm grasp.

"Your father needs to know about the doctor," she said.

Tommy was silent, waiting.

"Now you go over there and yell to your father the doctor's been called. You hear?"

"Yes'm." He pulled his hand free and jumped from the step.

"And you come directly back!" He was running and the sun flashed in his blond hair. "Tommy, you mind me!" she shouted. "Don't you go up close!" He waved, but did not turn around.

When he got to the circle of men, Tommy Higgins stopped running. He walked slowly because the men were so quiet and kind of lonely looking. Something very serious was happening and the men were all respecting it. Juan, the Mexican, glanced at him as he stepped up but didn't smile or even raise his hand. Old Alf just squatted, one knee in the dust, and twisted his neck hair, his jaws working in that old man's way. It was all very still and respectful, like in a church, and all the men were just there, still and kind of empty.

His father's back was to him, hiding somebody there in the hay, and when he moved around, he saw it was Billy Parker. Billy was lying all stretched out but it was kind of funny like. The lower part of his body had been reduced somehow, as though the air had been let out of his legs and the legs were all kind of pushed up toward his belt. His arms lay along his sides and the hands seemed to touch too far down, as though they'd been stretched. Billy was very quiet and still and it was as if he was a model for the other men about how to do it, and they were all copying him or trying to but Billy was the best because no part of him was moving, not even his eyes.

"Pa?" Tommy said, not looking at his father.

"What are you doing, boy?" his father said.

"Ma sent me. She called Doc Mertins, like you said."

His father took his arm and shook him a little. "That's fine, Son. Now you go on back to your mother there." Higgins gave the boy a small shove and Tommy stumbled. "You go on back. This is no place for you."

"What is it, Pa?"

"You go back, hear?"

"Yessir."

"Go back to your mother."

Tommy retreated, his eyes full of Billy Parker stretched out in the yellow hay. When his father was satisfied Tommy was moving properly, he turned to give Billy another drink. Tommy stopped. He was next to old Alf, the swamper.

"What is it?" Tommy whispered.

The old man stopped his chewing motion and regarded the boy like a stranger. Tommy had known Alf and most of the other men all his life. Billy had helped him to learn how to ride and to shoot a twenty-two.

"Alf, what's wrong with him?"

The old man's eyes were white and veined, like cracked egg shells. His voice came out like powder. "Accident," he said. "Billy had a' accident."

Tommy stared at the man lying in the hay.

"Billy?"

"Tractor fell on him," old Alf said. "Tractor just rolled on him." He gestured with one wrinkled hand. "That's what did it there."

Tommy looked at Billy Parker and for the first time he noticed that both his feet were pointed the same way, like the feet of Emily Harker's rag doll when she laid it on the floor.

"The doctor will fix all that, won't he, Alf?"

The old man looked over to where the cattle were bunched around the trough. German Jim, who was squatting a few feet away, shook his head.

"No doctor goin' to fix what the tractor did, boy. No doctor."

The force of the communication was so strong that instinctively John Higgins turned about and saw his son standing there. He saw that the boy knew but he pretended he hadn't seen. "I thought I told you to get on to your mother."

"Yessir," Tommy said, retreating again.

"Get on back."

And then, as if only needing the boy's knowledge to break some final, invisible human link, Billy Parker screamed. The sound was like nothing Tommy Higgins had ever heard and he stopped, stiff with fright. Billy screamed again and the sound made John Higgins stand straight up because he had never heard such a sound, nor had any of the other men, except old Alf, who stared with large, broken eyes at the crushed man in the hay. The scream brought Mary Higgins running from the porch, hair flying, toward her young, terrified son. But there was no chance. Billy Parker died before she got half way there.

The evening had come on and in the old barn the summer air was heavy with dark and dust. The dead man lay under a horse blanket in one of the stalls.

Outside, the air was cool and bright. The crickets were going and over by the trough a few of the Hereford steers had not settled down. They raised soft rolls of dust that gathered and hung about their legs like fog. They smelled the damp green corn in the field to the east and they smelled the barn and their blunt white faces were open and still.

In the bunkhouse the men had finished eating. German Jim sat at the wooden table shuffling cards. Juan, the Mexican, was filling his pipe and whispering to himself. Old Alf, the swamper, had gathered Billy Parker's things and they lay in a little pile on the dead man's bunk.

All the lights were on at the big house and in the kitchen Mary Higgins was clearing the dinner dishes. "When will they be coming?" she asked.

Her husband looked up from the white tablecloth. "Soon, I expect. It's forty-five minutes to town."

"I don't understand why Doc Mertins couldn't have done it," she said.

"Now how was Doc Mertins going to do that in that little coupe car of his?"

"Well," she said.

"Anyway, the coroner has got to come. That's how they do it. That's what the doc said they do."

"Oh," said Mary. She picked up the bowl of red grapes and for the first time noticed her son's plate. "Tommy, you haven't eaten hardly a thing."

"I'm not too hungry, Mom," the boy said.

"You should eat," she said.

His father looked at the boy's plate and he too seemed to be just aware of it. "Eat," he said.

"But Pa, I'm not hungry."

"You should keep up your strength, young man," said his mother.

"Your mother's right, Son. Eat something. Get some of those greens down you. There's chores tomorrow."

The boy touched the mashed potatoes with the point of his knife.

"That's all good food, young man, and I don't want it to go to waste."

"Waste not, want not," said John Higgins.

"You know the rule," said his wife. "You don't clean your plate, you don't get any dessert."

"I don't want any dessert, Mom."

"Then you don't get up from the table. You know the whole rule."

"Yes'm." The boy touched the meat with his fork.

They were silent. The man and woman watched the boy cut the meat slowly. Tommy Higgins watched the knife moving back and forth.

"My pa did the same thing," John Higgins said. "Made us kids always clean our plates. Always had to."

Tommy raised a small slice and put it into his mouth. He chewed slowly.

"Helps you sleep," Mary Higgins said. "A good meal helps you sleep."

The boy was eating and the silence came down again, like a jar. The man looked at the white tablecloth and the woman picked up a few more things and went to the sink. Then there was only the sound of the boy eating and the movement of his eating.

"And there are poor people all over the world without anything," Mary Higgins said.

After a few moments John Higgins said, "I expect I'd better go outside. I'd better be out there. I'd better be with the men."

"Can I go, Pa?" Tommy said.

"No!" he said. Mary turned around. There were tiny scars of fear struggling in her face. John Higgins softened his voice. "No, Son," he said. "Now you stay here and help your mother."

The boy said nothing.

"You help her with the dishes or something."

"I never help her with the dishes, Pa."

"Then get to your homework for school."

"Tomorrow's Saturday. I'll do it on Sunday."

"Well, get up and do it now."

"Billy was my friend, Pa." The boy was almost crying.

John Higgins swallowed and reached out to touch his son. But his hand stopped and the fingers shook. The hand hung in the air and trembled like a big, clumsy spider.

"Well, that's over now, Son. That's just over. Billy was a good man, a good worker—"

"He was a Christian man too," Mary Higgins added quickly.

"Anyway, that's over."

"I don't understand, Pa."

"There just was an accident," the woman said.

"Those things happen sometimes," John Higgins said. "Now you stay with your mother.

Mary Higgins held one hand in the other and stared over the table at the wall, where the cheap picture of a field of orange flowers was hung.

"The men were all laughing and gay this morning when you all went off. We were going to the movies together tonight, the three of us. And now this thing has happened. I'll be glad when they come and take it away."

She turned, walked back to the sink and plunged her hands into the soapy water. She felt strangely angry at Billy Parker for what he had done, and the anger made her ashamed and guilty and she hung her head.

"I'd better be with the men," John Higgins said, standing. "I guess I ought to be there when they come."

No one said anything and so John Higgins went outside.

The dead man lay under the blanket in the dark. The barn rose up and surrounded him, like a cathedral of deeper dark, so that the night outside the high, open doors appeared too vast, too far away, too different to be real.

Elmer, the old sheep dog, came into the barn once, curled his tail and slunk away. The dead man had had no other visitors. Even the flies were absent, asleep in cracks and edges of the barn, their enormous energy quieted by the cool air. A perfect, unchallenged stillness covered the man in the stall, like that of the vague lumps of machinery and hay arranged upon the concrete floor. The blanket swelled a little with the dead man's dying.

A figure appeared at the door, its silhouette making a black hole in the night sky. It hesitated, the starlight bursting beyond it, and then, in a kind of osmosis, moved from one darkness into the other. It stood, waiting and listening, and then came over to the stall.

Tommy Higgins knelt down five feet from Billy Parker. That's who it was there under the heavy blanket. It was Billy

Parker, with the air out of his legs and his hands too far down and his feet still turned the same way. It was his friend Billy. It was Billy Parker.

Tommy had crawled under woolen blankets in the winter time to sleep. In the dark under the blankets it was hot and thick and it was like the wool was in his lungs and he couldn't breathe. He wondered if that's what it was for Billy there in the stall, hot and thick and wool in his lungs except he couldn't breathe at all.

Billy was dead. Ever since that scream had faded away, shattering the air as far as it reached, Billy was dead. He was dead afterward and then later and then during dinner and he was still dead now. He was there dead in the stall with the blanket over him.

Tommy opened his mouth and then closed it. He had wanted to ask Billy a question and it was almost as if he could ask it and Billy would answer. He knew Billy had the answer. He knew he could explain it the way he had explained about the twenty-two and about riding. Billy was that kind of man. He would have explained it.

Tommy remembered the dog they had owned before Elmer. It was a chow named Tippy and he had found Tippy one afternoon under the rear axle of the old Chevy, its legs kind of stiff and its eyes bright and open and the flies dancing in the sunlight. He had cried because of Tippy but it was all right. It was not all right that Tippy had died but it was all right for him because of what his mother did and his father bought him a new dog. And it was all right.

But now Billy Parker's scream echoed in Tommy's head, breaking the fibres between thoughts, leaving them separate and confused. The one who could tell him was lying there under the wool blanket. Billy was just there in the horse stall and could offer nothing but the crushed lump of himself, so that Tommy even wondered if maybe it wasn't Billy Parker at all.

Then a car sounded in the driveway and there was the flash of its lights. Tommy jumped up. He heard the bunkhouse screen door bang open and his father's voice. There was nothing else for him to do. He ran behind the bales of hay. The car stopped right in front of the open barn doors and two men got out. He saw his father and the hired men come up and his father shook hands with the two from the car. Then they all came into the barn.

"Juan, catch the lights," John Higgins said. His voice had that direct authority of one who owns others.

The lights came on, naked bulbs strung here and there about the rafters and beams. They looked like yellow blooms growing in the thick darkness. One spread itself just above the stall where Billy Parker lay.

"Well, it's too bad," one of the men from the car said. "He was a nice fella, Billy was."

The men nodded and shuffled their feet. They all watched the lump under the blanket.

"He was a good worker," John Higgins said. "Wasn't he, boys?"

They nodded. Old Alf sucked on his cheeks and looked over to where Tommy was peeking through the bales of hay. He looked right at the place where Tommy was hiding but didn't see him. His old man's face was wrinkled with life and Tommy stared at it the way he stared at the preacher's face on Sunday, but then Alf spat into the dust and turned away. Tommy drew back and lowered his eyes.

"Tractor, you say," the man said.

"Yes," said John Higgins.

"How'd it happen?"

"Got the right rear tire into a ditch and the thing just went over."

"Just like that."

"Took him right with it."

The other man in the car, who had not said a word except to shake hands, clucked his tongue. Juan, the Mexican, blessed himself and glanced away from the stall.

"Well, accidents happen, John. You can't stop the way things happen."

"Now, you can't do that."

"Workin' on a farm, with machinery, you got to expect

things'll happen. You don't want them to, but they do. At least the poor devil didn't suffer much."

"No, he went pretty quick."

"I seen worse. It ain't the worst way to die. I seen worse than this. Over in Coulterville last week. That Barton fellow, remember? The fork lift truck accident?"

"I read about it."

"I seen a lot worse than this."

"I guess it happens to all of us."

"There's worse ways to die. I'm not too sure it wasn't all right. We can't all die in bed. Maybe it's even better this way. Who knows? You can see what you're dealing with. I seen a lot of people die and a lot more dead and I haven't figured it out."

"It's God's will," said John Higgins.

"Why would God will anything like this?" the man asked.

They were quiet for a few moments, staring down at the shape on the floor.

"Well," the man said, "guess I'd better have a look."

He bent down and pulled the blanket back. The men leaned forward and in the petals of yellow light they all stared with blunt, open faces at the dead man.

"Did he have any kin?" the man asked.

"He didn't have any that I know of. Boys?"

No one answered.

"All right. Well, the county will take care of things. Do you want to do anything for him?"

John Higgins looked at his men. "Well, we ought to do something."

The others looked away shyly.

"Well, there are some papers and things, John. Can you come in and take care of that?"

"I'll be in Monday morning."

"That'll be fine, John. We can take care of everything then. Now if you boys will help me here, we'll just put the body in the back of the van and be on our way."

There was a soft flutter of uncertainty and then hands went down into the stall and came back up with the body of Billy

Parker. The men moved out into the night and the man who had clucked his tongue opened the door of the van and the hands all went in and then came out empty. The man slammed the door and went around to the other side.

"Well, I'm sorry all this had to happen, John. I know how things like this can interrupt routine and work and all. But they happen. That's life, you know. How's the ranch doing?"

"Oh, fine, Jeb, fine. Good corn crop this year. Cattle are fat. It'll be a good year."

"Well, work's a blessing," the coroner said, starting the engine. "Say hello to the missus for me and I'll see you Monday morning."

"Fine. Good night."

The engine started. The lights came on. The van drove away.

John Higgins turned to his men. "Alf," he said, "you and the boys take what you want from Billy's things. I guess you can just throw the rest out. I'll catch the switch in the barn."

The men moved toward the bunkhouse. John Higgins went into the barn, glanced about and then switched out the lights. He walked toward the main house, leaving a thin, lifting trail of dust behind him.

In the still dark of the barn, Tommy Higgins was crying. He had to wait until his father got into the house and was settled before he could sneak back through the bedroom window. He came out from behind the bales of hay and went over to the stall where Billy had been. Only the blanket was there, crumpled and flat, as though the air had been let out of it.

What was it that was frightening him so? What had been there and was now gone and was frightening him so? He wanted to run to the house, to rush to his bed and cover himself and be asleep, but he simply stood there, trembling and afraid, the tears streaming down his cheeks. There was something so terrifying and yet so special, pounding in the night all around him. It was so terrifying and so beautiful and so special that no life could ever go on again and yet it would go on. He would get up tomorrow morning and do his chores and Monday he would to to school.

He was alone in the dark. Not even the dead man was with him anymore. He opened his mouth as if to scream but no sound came. Something was all in the air about him, everywhere, something smothering and close so that he could scarcely breathe, something that had started that afternoon in the hay with Billy Parker. And then in the thunder and pulse of his black fear he knew what it was. It was the beating of his own heart.

August Heat

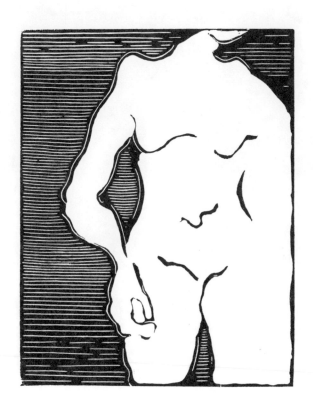

There had been a lot of rain that winter, over twice what was normal for the valley. Mushrooms were growing on the walnut tree at the Johnson place, which old man Johnson said was a sign the tree was getting ready to die. The farmers could do nothing because the land was like mush, and the worms came to the surface, where the jays and blackhawks got them. The gophers worked frantically in the wet loam and put up stippled mounds everywhere.

Then the wind came in from the north and blew the rain away. It blew the haze and fog away too, and you could see the snow on Mt. Diablo and the purple ridges in the foothills below. The snow was piled on the Sierras to the east and the mountains looked as though you could walk to them before noon.

The air began to change in February and Billy Harrigan noticed the difference. It took a sensitive man to feel it. It wasn't just that the days were a little longer, because the cold was still there. The frost came hard in the morning and the grass cracked when you walked on it and the fog returned and held thick and wet for days. It rained heavily again.

But the wind was different. There was a promise in the wind, and Billy would smell it in the waning afternoons and feel it under the cold heat of the February sun. He began riding Apache, his favorite ranch horse, into the foothills to the east, and when he came to a good spot he jumped from the horse, picked a blade of grass, put it under his tongue, and walked slowly and easily along, studying the blue film over the valley.

It was there in his mind, then, summer, with all the leaves out and the breeze sweet in the limp, tall grass. He liked the August heat and having his shirt off and doing heavy, hot work with his hands. He liked sweating and the taste of it in his mouth and the taste of a cold beer or even two or three beers. He liked the deep, strong fatigue in his back and arms after a bath and the smell of a clean shirt and the talk with the other men in the still evenings. And he liked going to bed naked with just a sheet and the window open so that he could smell the fields and hear the ranch falling asleep. He liked the warm privacy of summer sleep.

Mae Johnson was crazy about horses and that's why she liked the summer. During the winter months she spent long hours in the tackle room cleaning and oiling the riding gear. She curried the horses, kept the frogs of their hooves clean, and fed them warm mash. She petted and talked to the horses as though they were children.

There was a wildness in Mae. She often rode horseback across the fields, shouting at the animal to go faster, faster, beating at the horse's flanks with her tiny heels until, by summer's end, they were as callused and hard on the inside as Billy Harrigan's hands. She liked fun and often drove one of the trucks into Jackson on Saturday night to eat dinner and dance at Miller's Place. She always wore faded blue Levi's and a flannel or cotton shirt. The only times she put on a dress were when they went to visit friends in Stockton and go dancing at the Trianon Ballroom. Billy was quiet, did not dance, and kept to himself. That was why Mae did not pay him attention until the third year of his joining the ranch.

Old Ira Johnson liked Billy for those very qualities Mae did not appreciate. Billy was a hard worker, one of the hardest the old man had ever known, and he was quiet and minded his own business. But there was another quality about Billy that Ira admired. It was an almost intuitive understanding of the earth and what it could do. He never had to tell Billy anything. Billy knew. He knew often before the old man himself, and this pleased Ira so much that in that third year, when Carl Hayes, his foreman, quit for a job up north, he asked Billy to take over.

Billy did not know what to do. He had never had much motivation in that direction, on this place or any other, and in fact enjoyed simply being a ranch hand with the rest of the men. He had a hard time deciding, which hurt the old man. Billy saw this and it made it all the harder, because he liked Ira and respected him. Ira decided to clinch things by welcoming Billy more warmly into his own family. He began having Billy to supper.

There were only the two of them, of course, the old man and Mae. Ira's wife had died of cancer when Mae was only five, and he had never remarried. The first time Billy came to supper, Mae laughed at him so much that his face turned red and he left the table. Ira chewed her out good for that, which was more for his own feelings, because he had absolutely no control over her.

"But, Pop," she laughed, her blue eyes catching the light, "he's so damned clumsy. He must've dropped his fork five times."

"He's not a clumsy man, Mae. He was just embarrassed."

"What's he got to be embarrassed about, I'd like to know?"

"Lord, girl, all you have to do is be kind to the man. He's just shy, that's all. He's a shy man who's trying to make up his mind."

"Seems to me a man that clumsy'd have a hard time managing anything, let alone a ranch."

"I wouldn't be too quick to be critical," Ira said. "There's a lot in that boy. Never saw a better man with ranchin'." He winked at his daughter. "Maybe it's you he's nervous about."

Mae laughed. "You sly fox," she said. "So that's the reason you're having him to supper, is it?"

"And that's why I'm asking him for tomorrow night too, so fix something special and be nice." His face turned serious and he placed one vein-twisted hand upon hers. "You know I'd like to see you married off pretty soon anyway, daughter. If not to Billy, then to some nice fella like him. My time will come one of these days, and then this whole place will be yours. You'll need a man then."

"Oh, Pop!" Mae laughed. "You're too obnoxious to die. This all sounds like one of those movies."

"I know, I know," he said, "but anyway — a man's time comes, and he'd like to have a little security and peace of mind about things."

The following night Mae did not laugh at Billy. Instead she studied him. He was tall, slender. He was losing his hair, and there was a little wispy tuft of it just above his forehead. He had a large Adam's apple, large wristbones and hands. He had a soft, smooth voice and restless eyes. She decided he wasn't so bad looking but not really her type. Billy would probably be content to sit in front of the TV on Saturday night or read magazines. That wasn't fun.

Fun was someone like Ben Yaddow, whom she'd been seeing pretty regularly lately. Ben drove a logging truck for Wilson Paper Company, and he was strong and quick and a good dancer. She liked very much the way Ben kissed her. She liked it so much that she was deciding to go all the way with him, which she did with every man she really liked. She never had any conscience about it, since it seemed as natural and as instinctively part of her free nature as dancing or riding fast horses. But, then, Billy might be fun to tease a little and she had promised to be friendly for her father's sake.

They went for a picnic that Sunday in the foothills. The sun was out, promising spring, and there was no wind. Mae packed a lunch of ham sandwiches, potato salad, beer, and chocolate cake. Billy got the horses ready. They found a large oak tree and Billy spread the table cloth and they sat down.

"It's nice up here, isn't it, Billy?" she said, passing him a sandwich.

"Yes, it is," he said. "I always liked riding up here."

"Do you do this often?"

He was embarrassed.

"What's the matter?" she laughed. "We have to talk, don't we? Here, have a beer."

"I don't mind talking," he said.

She smiled warmly. "Pop is sure hoping you'll be our new foreman. Have you made up your mind yet, Billy?"

He looked across the valley and a light came into his eyes. She followed his gaze but only saw the flat green land and the distant coast range mountains.

"I'm making up my mind," he said. "It's hard."

She swallowed from her beer can. "I'd think you'd jump at the chance. Means a big raise in pay and you'd get to boss things. Most men'd give their eye teeth for that."

"I know," Billy said, "and I'm much obliged to your father for asking me. Your father's a fine man to work for. Lets a fella alone to find his own way."

Mae looked carefully at Billy. There was something here she hadn't noticed before, something mysterious. It forced her to think a little about herself. She didn't like thinking, not because she was afraid but simply because it never seemed to matter.

"What's keeping you from deciding?" she asked.

He looked at her. "Don't know. A feeling, I guess."

"You aren't afraid of the responsibility, are you?"

"No, I'm not afraid of that."

"Well, of what, then?"

"I don't know as I'd call it afraid."

"What is it, then?"

"It's me, just me," he said.

She looked at him, puzzled. Now he had begun to intrigue her, which was interesting too. She decided that she liked this

Billy Harrigan, that he might be nice to have around to talk to when she was sick or bored or something. Besides, he liked horses.

"You're sort of strange," she said after a moment, "but I like you, Billy. You're honest too, aren't you? If you could stay, I think it would be a good thing. I didn't think so at first, but I think now you'd make a good foreman." She placed a hand on his shoulder. "I hope you'll stay too. And so I'm officially asking you. I hope you'll stay and be foreman, Billy."

He reddened and she laughed and brushed a quick kiss against his cheek.

"You're not so shy," she said, "you're just serious, aren't you? You're one of the serious ones. It's so easy to embarrass you, you'll have to watch out. There's a mean streak in me, and I'll be after embarrassing you all the time, Billy Harrigan."

He shook his head and laughed, and it was the loudest, gayest laugh she had ever heard, and she put her head against his shoulder and laughed and laughed until the tears came to her eyes.

It was the beginning of March before Billy made up his mind. The almond trees had thrown their blooms and the bees swarmed hungrily through them. The tractors were busy in the fields and the gulls bunched in the wet furrows. The earth turned its belly to the sun.

Billy rode Apache often into the foothills to study the great valley. There was so much openness, so much flat, reaching openness that he felt compelled to leave, to go somewhere, to do something and yet he stayed, and he knew he was going to stay, he was only trying to get clear of a feeling about staying.

Mae watched him from the house and sometimes went with him. She wondered about Billy and was interested in him and a little troubled by him. Old Man Johnson was desperate, until one night at supper Billy smiled and said he'd take the job.

"Say!" Ira exclaimed. "Now your're talking, Billy." He reached over the table and shook Billy's hand.

"It's a fine opportunity, Ira," he said. "I'll do my best to live up to your expectations."

"I'm not concerned there, son," said Ira. "You know how I feel about you. You're the best fella I've seen with a ranch. What do you say, Mae?"

"I think it's real fine, Billy. The ranch will be in tip-top shape with you here."

"Aren't you just pleased a little, Mae?" He winked at Billy.

"Sure I am, Pop," she smiled. "Now you cut that out. "Look, *you're* embarrassing Billy this time."

In fact Billy had dropped his eyes. A patch of red had formed on each cheek.

"Say," Ira said, "I'm going out to tell the other men. Might as well get things started as of right now. Start everything off proper tomorrow morning."

When the old man left, Mae refilled Billy's coffee cup. They sat there quietly a few moments. Billy wiped the palms of his hands with his napkin.

"So you're staying, Billy," she said.

"Yes," he said.

"What made you finally decide?"

"I don't know."

"That's a funny answer, Billy."

"I guess maybe it is," he said. "I guess maybe I just felt I had to stay. Your father has been so right by me and all."

Then she felt like teasing him again. "And did you stay for me a little too, Billy, because I asked you?"

He blushed deeply and turned his face away. "Yes," he said.

She sat back in the chair and looked carefully at him. She felt a little weak and then grew angry. Her heart began to pound with anger because there was no weakness in her and it must be coming from him. There was a weakness in him concerning women and she did not like the feeling it gave her.

"Well, I'm glad you're staying, Billy," she said. "The ranch really needs a man like you. I've got to get to these dishes now, if you'll excuse me."

She stood up and began clearing the plates away. He sat there, a perplexed look on his face.

After he told the men about Billy, Ira went over to the barn to smoke and think. He was very excited and nervous. He had almost given up hope and now here it was. Billy was going to stay after all. He was going to be foreman. That was over and settled and he could relax about that. Now if only he could get settled about Mae.

In the following weeks Ira worked hard on his daughter. Billy came to dinner often and during the day the old man hovered about Mae, prodding and suggesting and talking about Billy.

Mae did not respond to these efforts, and one afternoon Ira decided to talk to Ben Yaddow.

Ben lived in a trailer court in Jackson. He was a tall, strong man, proud of that strength and what it could do. A sense of physical grace surrounded everything Ben did, and even the old man felt it that day when he told Ben about his idea. Ben laughed and laughed. He thought it was some kind of joke. But when he looked into Ira's white face and the pale, liquid eyes that would not meet his own, he knew the old man was not joking. Then Ben began to think.

The whole thing was queer and the feeling of queerness made the flesh along his spine move and the thinking did no good because he could not understand, but that wouldn't make any difference anyway. When Ira said that he'd add another five hundred, Ben thought of Big Sur, where he'd recently been wanting to go. He looked at the old man and then stuck out his hand. Ira took it. Ben gripped the hand and commenced to pump it hard up and down. He laughed and pumped the hand and Ira could only leave it there. His entire body loosened and he felt as if something had taken hold of his heart and was squeezing the life away.

Spring came. Poppies sprouted in the fields and along the roads. The wind blew the clouds away. In great white puffs they sailed low to the ground, their dark shadows racing after them. The grass grew heavy and green under the warm, white sun.

When Mae discovered she was pregnant, she locked herself in her room, took off all her clothes, and examined her body in the full-length mirror. Her body was like that of a thoroughbred, made for racing, alert, eager, and yet sensitive. And now something had entered her. She could feel the slow seed growing. Something had gone wrong with the protection, that was it. She had been careless about examining the protection. It was her own damned fault, that was all.

She pressed her hands against her stomach, and a strange, hot desire flamed in her breasts. She blinked her eyes. She would not tell Ben, did not want any man held to her in that way. She would just give the kid away. That was the simplest thing, just dump the kid. Let somebody else who loved kids have it. Then she sat down on the bed and cried.

She did her best to conceal the pregnancy. She took to wearing dresses and got a lot of good-natured kidding from the ranch hands. She did not go into Jackson for fear of seeing Ben, and when she heard he had left town, she thought it was just as well, it was the way she wanted it. She would have the kid and everything would be all right again. Then she realized that, even with Ben gone, she did not much want to go dancing. She did not much want to do anything. And when she looked in the mirror lately, there was the swelling and she realized for the first time that a life was building itself in her body. Out of the material of her flesh, a life was being formed, like an arm or a leg, building itself out of her energy and pride. It was as much her body as her body was.

Every day now, several times a day she looked at her naked body in the mirror. My God, she thought, look at me, look at that! She marveled at the thing she had not willed which was in some crazy way leeching the anger from her. She began to want the kid, to want it the way she wanted her own hands and feet, and she felt guilty. A deep shame touched the center of her heart, for what she wanted now had not been conceived in love but in the mistaken carelessness of muscle and

bone. Now she wanted the child and was afraid of the child
and afraid of the terrible burden of her becoming.

She wandered about her father, then, hovered about him
as a kind of magnetic, polar power. She could not tell him
and yet he would know soon, and she wanted to tell him. She
sought strength from him, petted him and teased him and
muttered with a peculiar, sweet breath about the cattle in the
fields and the taste of cold water from the spring. She sweated
a little on her upper lip and was proud and weak and drained
of lust. Her eyes grew larger. Every part of her seemed to be
growing, stretching and growing, as though it had to encom-
pass more life to feed the root of life growing in her. But Ira
was like an old stump. She sighed and touched her tongue to
her full lips. She felt her breasts and moved about him like a
caress, but he could not feed her.

"You spend too much time in this place, Mae," Ira said one
day. He stared out the window, watching Billy work by the
barn. "Why don't you ride horses or go to a dance or something?"

"I don't feel like any of that right now, Pop." She smiled.

"You not want to ride horses or go dancing? Something
wrong with you? Tell your old man."

"No, Pop, I'm all right."

"I like having you around, though, honey. I tell you, I like
it."

She smiled and felt just a little embarrassed.

"I always wanted us to be closer, Mae, and sort of live better together."

"I know, Pop."

He kept gazing at Billy through the window. "I'm just an
old man," he said quietly, "just an old man trying to make
sense of his last days. Can you blame me for that, Mae?"

"Of course not, Pop." She stood and walked over to him.
"Are you all right?"

"Sure, Mae, sure. Just watching Billy out there." She fol-
lowed his glance. "That boy works hard, Mae, and loves it.
He's a good boy." He did not look at her. "Talk to him, Mae.
He works so damned hard for us. He has good feelings about

things. He'd understand your feelings. He likes you too, Mae. He never says anything but he likes you. I'm just an old man who needs to rest. Forgive me."

That night after supper she went walking with Billy. Some of the men were sitting on the steps of the bunkhouse. One of the men was playing a guitar, and the notes floated like petals on the night air. The air was sweet with the perfume of the fields and the stars hovered against the darkness like hungry bees. Billy thought about the men at the bunkhouse. He knew all they would be talking about, for he had talked about it all himself many times and never grown tired of the talking. Equipment talk, work talk, complaining talk, bragging talk, women talk and, best of all, the talk of loneliness, the melancholy of lost, lonely men. He liked that, there was a capacity in that, a constant possibility and hunger outward about that. And when he had become foreman, the men had looked at him out of that melancholy as if to say, look what you've done, Billy, look what you've done, and he had become a homecoming to that hunger.

"It's a nice night, Billy."

"Yes, it is."

"I like nights like this, don't you?"

"Yes."

"These nights are the best of all."

He did not say anything. They bumped together as they stepped along, and he took her hand. It was a natural thing, but it was the first time he had ever deliberately touched her. He held her hand and they walked and there was a warm quiet in the air.

"Do you like being foreman, Billy?" Mae asked.

"It's hard work," he said.

"Pop says you're the hardest-working man he's ever seen."

"Well, I don't know about that," he said, full of pride.

She squeezed his hand. "I've watched you, Billy Harrigan. You make me tired just watching you. Why do you do that, work so hard I mean?"

"I don't know," he said, hurt by his impotence with words. "It's just a good thing to do. It gives me a good feeling."

"And about being foreman, Billy, does that give you a good feeling?"

He thought a moment. "It's a different kind of feeling. It's a feeling like—" He stopped and searched his mind. "It's a feeling like being somewhere you've always wondered about being in and then you're there and sort of just looking around."

"Like belonging to something important maybe but being afraid of it a little?"

"Maybe," he said. "Yes, it's some like that."

She stood before him. A yielding softness and warmth filled her body. He thought of her like the bread she baked, fresh from the oven, sweet smelling and ready, a promise of taste and desire. He had known some women in his life, as one knows a pair of gloves he does not intend to buy. But Mae was like something you've always wondered about, like the promise of wondering. She was like oven bread setting in a white, clean kitchen, and you came and waited in the place that wasn't yours, and wondered.

Billy knew he was going to kiss her and he put his hands on her arms and thought for a moment. Then he bent down and found her soft mouth. And then Mae placed her head against his chest and began to cry.

"What's the matter, Mae?" he asked.

"I—I'm ashamed," she said. "I'm doing something terrible. Oh, Billy, I got a terrible thing to tell you."

He held her away and tried to focus more clearly on her face. "Did I do something?" he asked.

"No, no, it's me. I was going to trick you, but I can't. I was going to get you to marry me, Billy. I'm pregnant and I need a father to have my baby the proper way. I was going to trick you, Billy. But I'm pregnant and I don't love the man and he's gone anyway. I want what's growing inside me and you're the best man I know, Billy. You're the kind of man I'd want that way. And so I'm asking you now plain out and honest and simple. Would you marry me, Billy?"

He dropped his hands and moved away from her. He looked across the darkened fields. He could feel the soft night wind from the north and then he felt something in him lift and float away, and it was gone and he was there under the lonely stars.

"I'll marry you," he said.

She moved next to him and touched him as one touches a sleeping animal to be sure it's alive. "Billy—"

"I was going to ask you anyway," he said. "In my time I would have asked you."

"Oh, Billy," she said, "what have I done? What have I done?'

After awhile he said, "It's all right. I've done it. Once I make up my mind to something, I make it up all the way. I was going to ask you anyway."

She looked at him with admiration and quiet fear.

The summer came. Mae grew larger. Everything in her slowed and became ready. She felt the heat of summer deep in her body, as though the child itself were reaching for the sun. She liked being slow and full of life and knew she would want other children, but she thought about riding horses and how she would have to get back to that right away after the baby, and she thought of Miller's Place and the Trianon Ballroom. She would go dancing again. She would teach Billy about dancing. He would learn for her sake. She would ride horses wildly and dance until very late. It would all be free and exciting again. When she thought this way, she could feel something breaking in her. All that summer she felt it breaking.

Billy worked very hard and the ranch bloomed under his hands. He realized he would have to work hard in the winter as well, for it was important to do the best job he could. He wasn't able to take any trips on Apache, and he did not talk to the ranch hands much anymore, and they came finally to see him as old man Johnson's son, and their conversation made the necessary adjustments. He stopped thinking about the valley.

Ira rocked alone on the front porch beneath the old walnut tree he had planted all those years ago. He felt anxious and confused and frightened and could do nothing but move the chair to the rhythm of the unforgiving hand that held his heart.

Then at last the walnut tree would no longer respond to water. It died all at once under the full, angry glory of that August heat.

Port of Call

W e were living in Stockton at the time, in a little house in the country. The house faced west and there was a lot of glass and in the evening the sunsets were beautiful. Quail ran through the yard and pheasants nested under the pine trees I planted. The grass grew tall and you could smell the water standing in the alfalfa fields across the road. We put out bird feeders.

Marian and I had been married fifteen years, and there were the kids. It was a relationship like most, starting out in college and ending with a diploma and a license. I don't know if we were in love. We petted a lot and then had sex in the back seat of the car, hidden behind the shrubs at the country club, and Marian cried when I said I wasn't sure if we should make it permanent. So I decided she would be a good mother for whatever children we might have, and though at the time I didn't realize it, I needed a mommy too. So we got married and went to Carmel and stayed in a motel. When we came back, I found a job teaching and we moved three or four times, the places always getting bigger and nicer, and we grew accustomed to each other. All my friends were doing the same thing.

One day in the dry heat toward the end of that fifteenth summer I drove into town to buy something, a shirt, a pair of pants, shoes—anything. I indulge myself like that whenever I get restless. The sun made rolls of shimmering light on the

gray asphalt and all around me was tall, limp-eared corn,
thickened barley, or blooming alfalfa. I felt momentarily, as I
looked up at the blue sky, as if there was a world, a universe
even, that had nothing to do with humans, that was totally
indifferent to their anxieties and dilemmas. It was a nice idea
to hold onto.

The men's shop where I buy all my stuff is located in Frank-
lin Village, the suburban bedroom community north of
Stockton where I teach. When I opened the door, I saw John
Fried, who owned the place, standing over the register kidding Sam Epstein. Sam was seventy and silver haired. He had
made a lot of money on the Filipinos in the old days, before
redevelopment closed down his dry goods shop on South
Center.

"Hey, Epstein," Sam said, smiling broadly and putting out
his pudgy hand, fingers spread apart. He called people by his
last name like that.

"Hello, Sam," I grinned. "Ya gettin' any?"

"Not me," he said, raising a finger to his lips. "Shhh. Too
old."

I laughed. "How's your wife feel about that?"

"Shhh," he said, touching my shoulder, "she's too old
too."

It was a regular routine we went through every time we saw
each other. Sam came in the store in the afternoon just to get
away from the house. He helped out, in his fashion, and once
in a while John gave him a sport coat or a pair of shoes. Not
that he needed the money. He made it big on those Filipinos
and paid eight hundred dollars a month for a condominium
with watchdogs and Japanese gardeners.

"What's doin', big Ted?" John said to me.

"Just kickin' around, John. You know me."

"Marian said it was okay," he grinned. "You can buy anything you want."

Hell, it was a regular vaudeville act. All we needed was a
juggler.

"Thanks for checking for me," I smiled, finishing it off.

Just then Dick Sanguinetti came up from the Cellar, where

all the casual pants and shirts were displayed. He was another owner, a kind of junior partner. Walking beside him was one of the loveliest women I had ever seen. My mouth opened.

"Hey, Teddy bear," he said, "what's up?"

"Oh, just kickin' around," I said, my eyes dancing from his face to the beautiful creature beside him. I checked out her left hand, a thing I'd found myself doing a lot lately. No ring. But she was married. I could tell she was married. She smiled at me and I saw the most exquisite thing I'd experienced all day.

"Have you met Joan?" Dick asked.

"No, I don't believe I have," I said, turning on my suave machine.

"I know you," she said. "We went to high school together. You were two years ahead of me, though." She cocked her head and looked at me out of the corners of her eyes. It fractured me.

"You went to Lodi High?" I asked.

"For the first two years," she said. "Then we moved to Stockton. You know, my son Terry certainly enjoys your writing class."

"Terry?" I said. "Are you Terry Billings's mother?"

"Yes." she smiled.

"Well, I'll be damned. He's a nice kid."

"He's a real hair," she said, laughing, "but I love him." Sam wandered off to the front of the store to talk to an old woman who had just entered. My eyes flicked to her left hand again. That third finger was absolutely naked.

She was so lovely, like one of those women out of *Vogue* or *Mademoiselle*—thirty-five, I guess, slender, dark haired, a strong angular chin. I had always had a prejudice for angular chins. Marian's was round and soft. I immediately had fantasies about her, like sitting in a quaint restaurant, sipping wine and pressing her knee under the table. She had small breasts and I cupped my hands over them in the quiet dark of a bedroom by the sea, scented candles burning, embers in the fireplace, the dull wash of the surf echoing against the walls. I've always been a romantic.

A soft ding-dong sounded. Someone had just passed through the electric eye at the rear door. Dick left to help.

"You've got quite a reputation, you know," the dark-haired goddess said.

"I do?" I asked, playing stupid because I knew what she was going to say.

"Yes, everyone knows what an excellent teacher Ted Harrison is."

"You're just trying to get Terry an *A*," I laughed.

"You teach a class at the junior college too, don't you?" she asked. "In the evening?"

"Yes."

"What's it called?"

"God and Man," I said.

"Oh, that sounds heavy."

"It's an existential approach to the god-man relationship," I said, turning professorial.

"Uh-huh." She grinned.

"Ooops!" I laughed.

We smiled at each other for awhile and I felt very warm and soft. I didn't know just what was going on inside me.

"I tried to get my older daughter Sandra to take one of your classes at the high school, but she couldn't fit one in, I guess. She graduated two years ago."

"Oh," I said, "I didn't know her."

"It certainly was her loss."

I blushed, just a little. I know my powers as a teacher. In fact, after my first couple years, I developed quite a following. I've tried to be objective about it, not let it go to my head and all, but hell, everybody likes to be stroked like that now and again, you know? I guess I just relate to kids.

John had listened quietly to all this but now he said, "Don't puff him up too much. He's bad enough to live with as it is."

"In fact," she said, "I just might take your course myself in the fall. I bet I could talk Andy and Bill into taking it too." Andy Barnes and Bill Dinibulo were salesmen at the Avenue branch of the store.

"The heck you could," I said, turning from her to John. "Say, is she real?" I asked. "I don't believe her."

She laughed and cocked her head at me again. A customer came in through the front door. "Excuse me," she said, walking toward him. I watched her go. She was wearing a pair of tight pants and everything moved so perfectly. I don't mean that lasciviously, you understand. She was sexy, all right. But she had a very gentle, giving quality about her that made me feel protective. She made me feel so damned good.

"Say, John," I said, "she's something else. I notice she's not wearing a ring. What's the deal?"

"I don't know," he said. "Her husband Frank was in that shooting accident a few years back. Remember that?"

"No," I said.

"Well, he's blind," John said.

I watched her move about, helping the middle-aged man who had come in. She seemed somehow almost like a girl of fifteen.

"It was in the paper," John said.

I nodded and just kept watching. I was in a cloud, a high, white cloud, and I knew I wouldn't come down for some time. "That's too bad," I said.

It was a week before I saw her again. Macy's was having a sale and I stood at a long counter rummaging through Arrow shirts. I looked up and saw her coming toward me. She wore one of those wide-brimmed hats, very chic and pulled over to one side, and a lightweight plaid suit, the jacket of which was cut like a man's. She wore round sun glasses and was even more stunning than when I'd seen her last.

"Hi," I said.

She stopped short and looked at me through those big dark glasses. She held her purse by a strap over her shoulder.

"Hello," she said. She stood, her feet close together and her hands crossed in front of her. She did not remove the glasses.

"Taking advantage of the sale?" I asked.

"Oh, just kicking around sort of," she smiled weakly. I began to think that something was wrong.

"I don't know why I come to these sales," I said, fingering one of the shirts. "I already have a million things."

"I know you have quite a wardrobe," she said, smiling, this time a little more warmly.

"Kids talking again, huh?" I laughed. "Actually, clothes are the only thing I really spend money on. I've always said John Fried is my only vice."

She laughed. "You're lucky, then."

"I suppose so," I said. I looked at her. Her lower lip was trembling ever so slightly. She did not stand erect but hunched over a little, as though carrying an invisible weight. "How long have you been working for John?" I asked.

"I just started," she said. "We went to Stockton High together when my family moved here. I was in the store one day shopping and he asked if I'd like to work on a part-time basis. I thought it would be fun to give it a try. Now that the kids are growing up, I enjoy getting out of the house."

"I like the idea of a woman working in a man's store," I said. "Most men have a hard time picking out their clothes."

It was just chatter, the kind of thing you go through when you meet people you don't expect to see again very soon.

"Well," she said, adjusting the strap of her purse. I threw the shirt on the counter.

"Say," I said, "let's go over to Lyons and have coffee. I'm in no particular hurry to get home."

She touched the rim of her glasses and was quiet a few moments. Then she said, "All right."

We walked out the west entrance of the store and across the huge parking lot to the restaurant. The sun was high and the air was warm. Tepid little sparrows danced up from the blacktop to rest on car fenders or thin, straggling trees, planted in square eruptions of earth. Then they flew down again to peck at spilled popcorn or the twisted wrappers from candy bars. We got to the front door and I held it open for her. We found a booth way over by the north corner and sat down facing Pacific Avenue. She took off her glasses and I saw that she had been crying.

"I didn't want you to notice," she said. "I just had to get

out of the house. You know how it goes."

"You had a fight with your husband," I said.

"Oh, it's beyond that," she sighed.

"Oh," I said.

We sat quietly for a few moments and the waitress came with the cups of coffee.

It's still so hard for me to describe how she made me feel, but this confession is certainly a part of it. There was an immediate openness that I found made the whole world around us sort of recede into a vacuous background. We sat huddled over our coffee cups and I started to talk. I told her about the family, not my own, the one I was raised in. About my old man's eighteen-year affair with another woman, for which I had always hated him so bitterly, where I went to college, and some of the things I'd done. She listened and I could see her relaxing as she explored my mind. The puffs under her eyes softened and went away. She was so beautiful, so rarely beautiful, her life just turning that corner or climbing that hill before moving slowly toward the end. She was at the time when a woman pauses and looks all around and says, "Where am I?" and "Who have I become?" and "What is left?" I sensed some great, sweeping adventure waiting for her, some book of destiny opening, and it was as though I could get in on the first page.

She told me about her children, about her husband's shooting accident, about how she had decided to go back to school and was now one semester away from finishing her sophomore year at the junior college. The waitress came again and again with fresh coffee. The sun moved over the sky and they lowered the blinds to keep out the glare. I sat next to the lovely, slender goddess and knew what was happening. We talked of high school, and common acquaintances rose, like icebergs in a blue sea, and we nudged them and pushed them aside and sailed on. She told me about her childhood, about her mother, who had been divorced twice, and her father, who lived in Seattle. She told me of how she and her husband had almost split up two years ago but had stayed together "for the kids." Slowly, in that blue sea, a continent began to emerge. I saw it as a broken line on the horizon. And then she said, "Guess what?"

"What?" I smiled, feeling as natural with her as with myself.

"I've talked Andy and Bill into it too."

"What?" I said.

"I'm taking your class in the fall. I think it starts in two weeks."

And there it was. Somewhere in that lifting continent, now white and mountainous before us, our ship was making for a hidden and quiet bay.

Of course, I should have gotten off right then and stayed in that other disquieting but familiar port. A lot of guys I knew were playing around, sleeping around. I don't want to seem clinical or prudish about this, but I'd been straight all my married life. The way I figure it now, it had a lot to do with my old man and the guilt about what he had done, but that protective racket can take you just so far, and that's usually to an emotional dead end. You spend fifteen years working at a job. You mow grass and get the car serviced and play golf at six forty-five in the morning. You take the kids to music lessons and read Saul Bellow behind the steering wheel or slump against the window waiting for them to be done. The wife gets a little heavy and frosts her hair and goes to encounter groups, and you get a little heavy and grow your hair over the collar of your shirt and buy patent leather shoes with raised heels. And there you are.

I felt I had run the limit with Marian, you know. She fit like an old bathrobe you keep around because you're used to it. She was the only woman with whom I had formed any kind of intimate relationship. The encounters before her were like kicking cans down a country road. All of which sounds like just another rationale for plain old ratting around, but really, I wanted to find out who I was with women. And though this may sound like a purposeless digression, it is absolutely essential to understanding how my life came to be floating about those days when I caught sight of that lovely dark-haired goddess.

I hailed a few ships before Joan in that year of self-discovery. There was Lori, red haired and wild, who chased me after I kidded her at a party. She enrolled in my college class and I succumbed to her charms one morning in early autumn. She scared the hell out of me, made me worried about getting caught, and relieved me by moving down south with her husband and three children. Then there was Marilyn, big breasted, the brown-haired wife of a psychiatrist, whom I kissed and fondled and drew back from, as one does from a tarantula, a creature also nice to admire, from a distance. And Jackie, a former student, whom I had on the banks of the Mokolumne River in pitch blackness while the mosquitoes affectionately caressed my bare parts. Not to mention a few women who, as I grew emboldened, ran from my passion after a fleeting touch, like gazelles from a lion. Because by the time Joan came along, I was totally convinced of what I had to offer, a fearless despoiler of women.

All of this is only a clever disguise for painful truths. My relationship with Marian had really gone sour. I didn't blame her completely. It was my fault too. It just seems that the child in me got hooked up with the parent in her and we were simply afraid to trust each other, to give to each other. We hung on like bulldogs and bounced apart and bounced together. The only time we really met was in bed, and that was like a cold shower, invigorating but not warming. Still, there were all the friends and the new house and transactional analysis and women's lib. And there were the kids.

So the new semester came around and that first night there she was, with Andy and Bill, sitting at a table in the corner, looking wistful and just a little sad. I outlined the course, talked about grading, and made an assignment, Dostoevsky's *Notes from the Underground*. Then I let the class go, since I hate lecturing. It was the first night anyway. I hung about for a bit talking, and when I turned around, all three of them were gone. I felt disappointed and went home.

The week dragged slowly by. I thought about her often and

even dropped into the store, but she was not working that day. The end of summer brought all the students back to school with deep, smooth tans, bright clothes, and funny stories. The days were warm and the kids lounged about, threw rainbow-colored Frisbees into the cloudless sky, or kissed furtively under the oak trees. It happened like that year after year.

Tuesday came around and I found myself eagerly anticipating the night. Marian and I had a terrible fight and threatened each other with divorce. It was a nice game and let off steam and meant we could get by without having to talk to each other for awhile. I drove into town and the sun was hot yellow in the western sky.

She was there, in a snug pair of red pants and a white doubleknit blouse. Her black hair was soft-curled about her shoulders and her brown-green eyes smiled warmly. I felt my heart beating. She set a tall thermos of coffee on the table before her. Andy and Bill, like quiet eunuchs, flanked her on either side.

And so I talked about underground man, that poor, suffering, spiteful, indecisive bastard, that broom-closet Hamlet. I talked about the pain of toothache, that pain that is mine and not yours, that proves how alone we are, that there is no system or code or ethic that can demonstrate to man what he ought to be. The words filled the air like an invisible smoke and the people inhaled. The demon of human desire and will was loosed among them and they sniffed and smelled at it, sitting as I did, in their complacent, middle-class underwear, missing *Bowling for Bucks* on the TV. And I looked at her and watched her and studied her.

An hour and fifteen minutes through the class, I gave the students a break. A lot of people left for the cafeteria. I walked over to the table and sat down.

"Very impressive." She smiled.

"Thanks," I said.

"Would you like some coffee?"

"Yes, I would."

She opened the thermos and poured me a cup. Andy and

Bill wandered outside to smoke.

"It's good how you get everybody to join in too," she said.

"It's no fun to talk to yourself," I said. I raised the cup to my lips and looked at her through the steam. "I've been wondering about you," I began. "Are you all right?"

She smiled without showing her teeth. "Same old thing," she said. "It's quiet now, though."

"That's the bang apart phase."

"Yes, the bang apart phase."

She looked at me with those big, brown-green eyes. They were soft and gentle and I found myself wondering how anyone could not love what I saw there. And then I felt foolish because I realized how Marian and I were hooked together, how blind we were to each other. Ironic, that for her, Joan, there should now be a double blindness. Maybe, I thought, people just can't see each other when they're young. Experience has a way of clearing the vision, though, if you let it.

We chatted quietly. I put out feelers. I told her how moved I was about our talk last week. She was moved too. I told her how good I felt about just opening up to her, straight out like that. She said she felt good about not having to be so protective. I told her that I wished things were different. She said she knew what I meant. Our eyes met and held and we both understood everything that was going on. I felt a little dizzy.

When the class came back, we talked about alienation for another hour and I let them go. As Joan got up to leave, I stepped over to her.

"Where's your car parked?" I asked.

"In the west lot, by the tennis courts," she said.

"Mind if I walk you out?" I asked.

"All right," she said.

We left the room and turned west. The old college campus was a large, sprawling thing and we had quite a walk to get to her car. I was in no hurry and moved along slowly. The stars were high and white and lovely. It felt very good just to be with her. When we got to her car, she asked if I'd like a lift back to mine, which was parked in the faculty lot. "Of course," I said, and off we went.

When we got to my VW, she stopped the car and I reached over very quickly and kissed her on the cheek.

"I want to see you again," I said.

She was momentarily surprised at my boldness, but then she said, "I'd like that."

Then I did a crazy thing. I gave her my address and told her why didn't she come out and we'd have coffee and talk. I picked Thursday morning, when I had a two-hour break between classes.

"I'll meet you then," she said, in a breathless whisper.

"Good night," I said.

"Good night."

My God, driving home I felt like Judas Iscariot. Here I was inviting a beautiful woman to my home for coffee and conversation, and we both knew we were going to get it on in my bedroom, with all the pictures on the walls and Marian's nightgown thrown across the back of a chair. I didn't like the thought of feeling guilty while enjoying my voyage of self-discovery. Yet it was all so modern. Joan was going back to school after all these years and we were beginning a relationship. It was part of the new things that were happening, and somehow sad and lonely because there was so little to hang on to but ourselves.

Out in the country now, I looked at the night through the windshield of the VW and smiled at myself. The trees, the grass, the weeds growing along the road, the farm animals lifting their torpid heads and staring emptily with marble eyes over barbed-wire fences, the dark itself, all the things my headlights illuminated were indifferent to my anxieties and my plans. That was my damned philosophic mind seeing the appropriateness of everything, a kind of cursed objectivity that even let me appreciate Marian's point of view and interrupted, every now and then, the metaphor of myself. There I was, plastering my subjectivity over the entire universe, enlivening it with this wealth of internal imagery, and then I understood what I was doing. Suddenly I saw myself lying under the earth and all this huge weight of darkness pressing down around me, only I didn't know anything because there was only dark and I was scared and I knew I had to have her and nothing mattered but that, and I'd take any guilt and anything else but I had to have her.

So Thursday came. I let my class out and drove home quickly. I walked dumbly about the house, and though Marian was at work, I was almost surprised not to find her there, brooding over a cup of coffee or looking accusingly at me under brass-colored curlers. I went into the bedroom and threw the covers back, being careful to see how they were arranged and just where the pajamas lay so that I could put it all back the same way. It seemed so Mephistophelian and coolly calculated that my heart began to beat wildly.

When she arrived, I opened the door and said, "Hi."

"Hello." She smiled, walked gingerly into the house, as though it were a museum. We went into the living room and sat down on the edge of the couch.

"Are you all right?" I asked, because I couldn't think of anything else to say.

"Yes," she replied, "and you?"

"Yes," I said, and then after a silence, "Joan."

"I know," she said, looking down, "I'm scared too."

With that I took her hand and we walked back to the bedroom.

"Kiss me first," she said.

I did, and it was so soft and good that I went weak. We removed our clothes, lay down on the bed, and made love for an hour and a half. And even though most of the time I was half listening for cars in the driveway or the sound of a doorknob turning, I knew my life was changed because I had never before experienced what I felt that morning. Joan got up, took a quick shower—being careful to use my towel—dressed, and hurried out the door. I kissed her good-bye and we made a date the following day for lunch. When she was gone, I rearranged the bed and looked under things for the wrong sized panties. Crazy, but that's how you are in a situation like that. I walked into the living room to catch my breath before starting back to school. I stood looking out the big glass windows at the pine trees.

It was so unusual, so out of the ordinary, that I had the peculiar feeling that it hadn't happened at all. It was only much later in our relationship that I was to understand that this was simply a part of how we were together. It only became real when we were joined and made it happen—and always it was fresh. With Marian I knew what to expect, when and how it would happen and what feelings of mine would not be used, sort of like frozen leftovers that never get eaten.

I now found myself entering an emotional no-man's-land. Everything with Joan was lovely and sweet. Everything with Marian was hard and empty. As the days and weeks passed, it was as though one woman were canceling out the other, a piece at a time. Joan's voice was softer, her laugh gayer, her smile open and warm. Joan's touch made Marian's clumsy and artificial. Joan's kiss made me turn my head away from Marian, and at night I slept as if alone on my side of the bed. Joan said the same thing was happening to her.

We tried to see each other as often as possible. We moved from coffeehouse to coffeehouse, restaurant to restaurant, looking for that one place where the eyes of strangers did not seem to grow familiar and knowing. Autumn came and went and all the trees grew bare. We met in Legion Park after school. Sometimes she fixed a lunch and we'd eat there at noon and watch the water. We'd throw a blanket on the grass and hold each other and kiss under the blue, cold sky. We stayed an extra hour after class on Tuesday nights and sat in her car on lonely, unlighted streets or grammar school parking lots, kissing and fogging the windows with our passion. I contrived excuses to go to town on the weekends so that I could drive by her house. We took a post office box and passed love notes and meeting places back and forth.

Then we began going to motels. I'd take a day off, saying I was sick, and we'd drive to Jackson or San Andreas and spend the day in bed, pausing in our lovemaking to drink wine and eat salami and Colomo French bread or take showers together. We made love and made love and made love, like people who had been starved all their lives, which, of course, we were. We took a couple of trips to the ocean together and I discovered the experience of awakening with someone I very much loved.

I guess that was what it was, but oh, how I fought it, how I struggled to keep from giving myself completely, and I could feel Joan struggling too. She fantasized a lot about our living together, how we would have satin sheets and never wear pajamas and have breakfast in bed and close the door on the whole world outside, as if afraid that someone or something might steal us away from each other. I felt protective about the relationship too. It all seemed so fragile and tenuous and maybe that was part of its beauty, you know—two people rushing toward each other in slow motion, arms spread wide and hungry. We were always like that.

One day, while we were sitting in the park watching the sun waves on the flat, clouded water, Joan said, "I don't believe in it anymore."

"What?" I asked, touching her raven hair.

"Any of it," she said. "The big house, the car, the kids, the swimming pool. I don't believe in any of it."

I looked away at the sky. I thought of my own family and felt how I seemed to be standing strangely beside them now rather than with them. "Yeah," I said.

"I've had all that and enjoyed all that, but I don't believe in it anymore. And I never really loved him, Ted."

Those times when we got so desperately serious thrilled me and yet made me apprehensive. And I didn't know whether it was some Oedipal flaw in my character or just a fear of the unknown. I wanted very much to start living with Joan right now, this minute, but the thought of having to inherit her children bothered me. And yet guys were doing it all the time. I wanted to think it was just a desire in me for independence. Maybe it was really a fear of all the tearing apart that had to come before new construction could begin.

"I guess we're going to have to do something," I said.

"We've both had affairs before," she said. "We both decided to, what you called it once—"

"Experiment."

"Yes. I don't need to experiment anymore, to find out who

I am by finding out who they are. I love you."

I nodded. Sometimes she held me like a small boy in the palms of her gentle hands. "I didn't know I was looking for love," I said.

"We've been looking for it all our lives, darling."

I swallowed and wet my lips. "I guess we have," I said. "I guess there's nothing else to look for."

"I guess there isn't."

I sat watching the water. I knew there would be no decision today, that the thought of it was all too immense for me to handle at the moment. Thinking, I had discovered, can be an actual curse. Thank God for Joan's wide heart!

"I guess it's time to go, darling," she said.

"Yes, you go on first. I'll see you tomorrow for lunch."

"Same place."

"Same time."

I kissed her deeply. Then I folded the blanket and handed it to her. She kissed me again and moved away over the rise of ground that protected the park from the street. Just before her head disappeared, she turned and waved and smiled. God, I loved her.

So I sat on a park bench and studied the quiet water. I realized that what I had walked into, almost by accident, casually, as it were, with a bit of the Don Juan about it, had turned into destiny or fate. That book that I had thought she was only just opening was my book as well.

I don't know. I guess there comes a time in every marriage when all the stuff comes floating to the surface, like wreckage from an ancient, sea-lost galleon, and it's like you don't even know the ship has gone down. For years the waves wash gravely and the tides run thickly. There are small storms. The cargo of hidden resentments shifts and little things tear loose and turn slowly upward. You look at them, you watch them. But the great ocean of routine is so vast and they are such tiny pieces, drifting there between work and music lessons, tiny little pieces of mind and heart that spin aimlessly, moved by sighs and long held breaths. Sometimes we speak of them, pointing them out curiously, wondering whether if they were only attached so and thus to the vessel, it would be seaworthy and might sail on and on forever. But that's because we don't know the ship has gone down and we are survivors. Those of us who don't know that float about the wreckage in self-made preservers, glad at least that it is our flotsam and our jetsam, or we patch and nail the whole thing as best we can with therapy and marriage counseling (after all, think of the kids). What we want simply is to stay afloat.

But for the rest of us there is the black storm, the heavens filling with terror, when the ship is torn asunder by a shotgun blast or a telephone call in the night from the wife of the man your woman has just screwed (confession is good for the guilty and lets you sail painfully on). The problem, you see, is what do you do when you realize the ship has sunk, the crew of emotions dead, and your misshapen, aging body (the hair just over the collar, the feet covered by soft patent) is floating face down in a lonely sea of junk? You look for round lights moving bayward in the sullen dark.

Whether or not my ship reaches that quiet port remains to be seen. I only know the wind is bellying the sails, the sky is blue, and the continent is growing tall and clear before me.

Sanchez

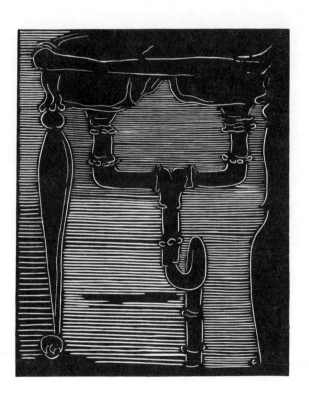

That summer the son of Juan Sanchez went to work for the Flotill Cannery in Stockton. Juan drove with him to the valley in the old Ford.

While they drove, the boy, whose name was Jesus, told him of the greatness of the cannery, of the great aluminum buildings, the marvelous machines, and the belts of cans that never stopped running. He told him of the building on one side of the road where the cans were made and how the cans ran in a metal tube across the road to the cannery. He described the food machines, the sanitary precautions. He laughed when he spoke of the labeling. His voice was serious about the money.

When they got to Stockton, Jesus directed him to the central district of town, the skidrow where the boy was to live while he worked for the Flotill. It was a cheap hotel on Center Street. The room smelled. There was a table with one chair. The floor was stained like the floor of a public urinal and the bed was soiled, as were the walls. There were no drapes on the windows. A pall spread out from the single light bulb overhead that was worked with a length of grimy string.

"I will not stay much in the room," Jesus said, seeing his father's face. "It is only for sleep. I will be working overtime too. There is also the entertainment."

Jesus led him from the room and they went out into the street. Next to the hotel there was a vacant lot where a building had stood. The hole which was left had that recent, peculiar look of uprootedness. There were the remains of the foundation, the broken flooring, and the cracked bricks of tired red to which the gray blotches of mortar clung like dried phlegm. But the ground had not yet taken on the opaqueness

of wear that the air and sun give it. It gleamed dully in the
light and held to itself where it had been torn, as earth does
behind a plow. Juan studied the hole for a time; then they
walked up Center Street to Main, passing other empty lots,
and then moved east toward Hunter Street. At the corner of
Hunter and Main a wrecking crew was at work. An iron ball
was suspended from the end of a cable and a tall machine
swung the ball up and back and then whipped it forward
against the building. The ball was very thick-looking, and
when it struck the wall the building trembled, spurted dust,
and seemed to cringe inward. The vertical lines of the building had gone awry. Juan shook each time the iron struck the
wall.

"They are tearing down the old buildings," Jesus explained. "Redevelopment," he pronounced. "Even my building is to go someday."

Juan looked at his son. "And what of the men?" he asked.
"Where do the men go when there are no buildings?"

Jesus, who was a head taller than his father, looked down at
him and then shrugged in that Mexican way, the head de-
scending and cocking while the shoulders rise as though on
puppet strings. *"Quien sabe?"*

"And the large building there?" Juan said, looking across
the rows of parked cars on Hunter Square. "The one whose
roof rubs the sky. Of what significance?"

"That is the new courthouse," Jesus said.

"There are no curtains on the windows."

"They do not put curtains on such windows," Jesus explained.

"No," Juan sighed, "that is true."

They walked north on Hunter past the new Bank of America and entered an old building. They stood to one side of the
entrance. Jesus smiled proudly and inhaled the stale air.

"This is the entertainment," he said.

Juan looked about. A bar was at his immediate left and a
bald man in a soiled apron stood behind it. Beyond the bar
there were many thick-wooded tables covered with green material. Men crouched over them and cone-shaped lights hung

low from the ceiling, casting broadening cones of light downward upon the men and tables. Smoke drifted and rolled in the light and pursued the men when they moved quickly. There was the breaking noise of balls striking together, the hard wooden rattle of the cues in the racks upon the wall, the hum slither of the scoring disks along the loose wires overhead, the explosive cursing of the men. The room was warm and dirty. Juan shook his head.

"I have become proficient at the game," Jesus said.

"This is the entertainment," Juan said, still moving his head.

Jesus turned and walked outside. Juan followed. The boy pointed across the parked cars past the courthouse to a marquee on Main Street.

"There are also motion pictures," Jesus said.

Juan had seen one movie as a young man working in the fields near Fresno. He had understood no English then. He sat with his friends in the leather seats that had gum under the arms and watched the images move upon the white canvas. The images were dressed in expensive clothes. There was laughing and dancing. One of the men did kissing with two very beautiful women, taking turns with each when the other was absent. This had embarrassed Juan, the embracing and unhesitating submission of the women with so many unfamiliar people to watch. Juan loved his wife, was very tender and gentle with her before she died. He never went to another motion picture, even after he had learned English, and this kept him from the Spanish films as well.

"We will go to the cannery now," Jesus said, taking his father's arm. "I will show you the machines."

Juan permitted himself to be led away, and they moved back past the bank to where the men were destroying the building. A ragged hole, like a wound, had been opened in the wall. Juan stopped and watched. The iron ball came forward tearing at the hole, enlarging it, exposing the empty interior space that had once been a room. The floor of the room teetered at a precarious angle. The wood was splintered and very dry in the noon light.

"I do not think I will go to the cannery," Juan said.

The boy looked at his father like a child who has made a toy out of string and bottle caps only to have it ignored.

"But it is honorable work," Jesus said, suspecting his father. "And it pays well."

"Honor," Juan said. "Honor is a serious matter. It is not a question of honor. You are a man now. All that is needed is a room and a job at the Flotill. Your father is tired, that is all."

"You are disappointed," Jesus said, hanging his head.

"No," Juan said, "I am beyond disappointment. You are my son. Now you have a place in the world. You have the Flotill."

Nothing more was said, and they walked to the car. Juan got in behind the wheel. Jesus stood beside the door, his arms at his sides, the fingers spread. Juan looked up at him. The boy's eyes were big.

"You are my son," Juan said, "and I love you. Do not have disappointment. I am not of the Flotill. Seeing the machines would make it worse. You understand, *niño?*"

"Si, Papa," Jesus said. He put a hand on his father's shoulder.

"It is a strange world, *niñito,*" Juan said.

"I will earn money. I will buy a red car and visit you. All in Twin Pines will be envious of the son of Sanchez, and they will say that Juan Sanchez has a son of purpose."

"Of course, Jesus *mio,*" Juan said. He bent and placed his lips against the boy's hand. "I will look for the bright car. I will write regardless." He smiled, showing yellowed teeth. "Goodbye, *querido,*" he said. He started the car, raced the engine once too high, and drove off up the street.

When Juan Sanchez returned to Twin Pines, he drove the old Ford to the top of Bear Mountain and pushed it over. He then proceeded systematically to burn all that was of importance to him, all that was of nostalgic value, and all else that meant nothing in itself, like the extra chest of drawers he had kept after his wife's death, the small table in the bedroom, and the faded mahogany stand in which he kept his pipe and tobacco and which sat next to the stuffed chair in the front room. He broke all the dishes, cups, plates, discarded all the cooking and eating utensils in the same way. The fire rose in the blue wind carrying dust wafers of ash in quick, breathless spirals and then released them in a panoply of diluted smoke, from which they drifted and spun and fell like burnt snow. The forks, knives, and spoons became very black with a flaky crust of oxidized metal. Then Juan burned his clothing, all that was unnecessary, and the smoke dampened and took on a thick smell. Finally he threw his wife's rosary into the flames. It was a cheap one, made of wood, and disappeared immediately. He went into his house then and lay down on the bed. He went to sleep.

When he awoke, it was dark and cool. He stepped outside, urinated, and then returned, shutting the door. The darkness was like a mammoth held breath, and he felt very awake listening to the beating of his heart. He knew he would not be able to sleep any more now, and so he lay awake thinking.

He thought of his village in Mexico, the baked clay of the small houses spread like little forts against the stillness of the bare mountains, the men with their great wide hats, their wide, white pants, and their naked brown-skinned feet, splayed against the fine dust of the road. He saw the village cistern and the women all so big and slow, always with child, enervated by the earth and the unbearable sun, the enervation passing into their very wombs like the heat from the yellow sun so that the wombs themselves bred quiet acceptance, slow, silent blood. The men walked bent as though carrying the air or sky, slept against the buildings in the shade like old dogs, ate dry, hot food that dried them inside and seemed to bake the moisture from the flesh, so that the men and women while still young had faces like eroded fields and fingers like stringy, empty stream beds. It was a hard land. It took the life of his father and mother before he was twelve and the life of his aunt, with whom he then lived, before he was sixteen.

When he was seventeen he went to Mexicali because he had heard much of America and the money to be obtained there. They took him in a truck with other men to work in the fields around Bakersfield, then in the fields near Fresno. On his return to Mexicali he met La Belleza, as he came to call her: loveliness. He married her when he was nineteen and she only fifteen. The following year she had a baby girl. It was still-born and the birth almost killed her, for the doctor said the passage was oversmall. The doctor cautioned him (warned him, really) La Belleza could not have children and live, and he went outside into the moonlight and wept.

He had heard much of the loveliness of the Sierra Nevada above what was called the Mother Lode, and because he feared the land, believed almost that it possessed the power to kill him—as it had killed his mother and father, his aunt, was in fact, slow killing so many of his people—he wanted to run away from it to the high white cold of the California mountains, where he believed his heart would grow, his blood run and, perhaps, the passage of La Belleza might open. Two years later he was taken in the trucks to Stockton in the San Joaquin Valley to pick tomatoes and he saw the Sierra Nevada above the Mother Lode.

It was from a distance, of course, and in the summer, so that there was no snow. But when he returned he told La Belleza about the blueness of the mountains in the warm, still dawn, the extension of them, the aristocracy of their unmoving height, and that they were only fifty miles away from where he had stood.

He worked very hard now and saved his money. He took La Belleza back to his village, where he owned the white clay house of his father. It was cheaper to live there while he waited, fearing the sun, the dust, and the dry, airless silence, for the money to accumulate. That fall La Belleza became pregnant again by an accident of passion and the pregnancy was very difficult. In the fifth month the doctor—who was an atheist—said that the baby would have to be taken or else the mother would die. The village priest, a very loud dramatic man—an educated man who took pleasure in striking a pose —proclaimed the wrath of God in the face of such sacrilege. It was the child who must live, the priest cried. The pregnancy must go on. There was the immortal soul of the child to consider. But Juan decided for the atheist doctor, who did take the child. La Belleza lost much blood. At one point her heart had stopped beating. When the child was torn from its mother and Juan saw that it was a boy, he ran out of the clay house of his father and up the dusty road straight into a hideous red moon. He cursed the earth, the sky. He cursed his village, himself, the soulless indifference of the burnt mountains. He cursed God.

Juan was very afraid now, and though it cost more money he had himself tied by the atheist doctor so that he could never again put the life of La Belleza in danger, for the next time, he knew with certainty, would kill her.

The following summer he went again on the trucks to the San Joaquin Valley. The mountains were still there, high and blue in the quiet dawn, turned to a milky pastel by the heat swirls and haze of midday. Sometimes at night he stepped outside the shacks in which the men were housed and faced the darkness. It was tragic to be so close to what you wanted, he would think, and be unable to possess it. So strong was the feeling in him, particularly during the hot, windless evenings, that he sometimes went with the other men into Stockton, where he stood on the street corners of skidrow and talked, though he did not get drunk on cheap wine or go to the whores, as did the other men. Nor did he fight.

They rode in old tilted trucks covered with canvas and sat on rude benches staring out over the slats of the tail gate. The white glare of headlights crawled up and lay upon them, waiting to pass. They stared over the whiteness. When the lights swept out and by, the glass of the side windows shone. Behind the windows sometimes there would be the ghost of an upturned face, before the darkness clamped shut. Also, if one of the men had a relative who lived in the area, there was the opportunity to ride in a car.

He had done so once. He had watched the headlights of the car pale, then whiten outward and the looks on the faces that seemed to float upon the whiteness of the light. The men sat forward, arms on knees, and looked over the glare into the darkness. After that he always rode in the trucks.

When he returned to his village after that season's harvest, he knew they could wait no longer. He purchased a dress of silk for La Belleza and in a secondhand store bought an American suit for himself. He had worked hard, sold his father's house, saved all his money, and on a bright day in early September they crossed the border at Mexicali and caught the Greyhound for Fresno.

Juan got up from his bed to go outside. He stood looking up at the stars. The stars were pinned to the darkness, uttering little flickering cries of light, and as always he was moved by the nearness and profusion of their agony. His mother had told him the stars were a kind of purgatory in which souls burned in cold, silent repentance. He had wondered after her death if the earth too were not a star burning in loneliness, and he could never look at them later without thinking this and believing that the earth must be the brightest of all stars. He walked over to the remains of the fire. A dull heat came from the ashes and a column of limp smoke rose and then bent against the night wind. He studied the ashes for a time and then looked over the tall pine shapes of the southern sky. It was there all right. He could feel the dry char of its heat, that deeper, dryer burning. He imagined it, of course. But it was there nevertheless. He went back into the cabin and lay down, but now his thoughts were only of La Belleza and the beautiful Sierra Nevada.

From Fresno all the way up the long valley to Stockton they had been full with pride and expectation. They had purchased oranges and chocolate bars and they ate them laughing. The other people on the bus looked at them, shook their heads and slept or read magazines. He and La Belleza gazed out the window at the land.

In Stockton they were helped by a man named Eugenio Mendez. Juan had met him while picking tomatoes in the delta. Eugenio had eight children and a very fat but very kind and tolerant wife named Anilla. He helped them find a cheap room off Center Street, where they stayed while determining their next course of action. Eugenio had access to a car, and it was he who drove them finally to the mountains.

It was a day like no other day in his life: to be sitting in the car with La Belleza, to be in this moving car with his Belleza heading straight toward the high, lovely mountains. The car was traveling from the flatness of the valley into the rolling brown swells of the foothills, where hundreds of deciduous and evergreen oaks grew, their puffball shapes still pictures of exploding holiday rockets, only green, but spreading up and out and then around and down in nearly perfect canopies. At Jackson the road turned and began an immediate, constant climb upward.

It was as though his dream about it had materialized. He had never seen so many trees, great with dignity: pines that had bark gray twisted and stringy like hemp; others whose bark resembled dry, flat ginger cookies fastened with black glue about a drum, and others whose bark pulled easily away; and those called redwoods, standing stiff and tall, amber-hued with straight rolls of bark as thick as his fist, flinging out high above great arms of green. And the earth, rich red, as though the blood of scores of Indians had just flowed there and dried. Dark patches of shadow stunned with light, blue flowers, orange flowers, birds, even deer. They saw them all on that first day.

"*A donde vamos?*" Eugenio had asked. "Where are we going?"

"*Bellisima,*" Juan replied. "Into much loveliness."

They did not reach Twin Pines that day. But on their return a week later they inquired in Jackson about the opportunity of buying land or a house in the mountains. The man, though surprised, told them of the sawmill town of Twin Pines, where there were houses for sale.

Their continued luck on that day precipitated the feeling in Juan that it was indeed the materialization of a dream. He had been able in all those years to save two thousand dollars and a man had a small shack for sale at the far edge of town. He looked carefully at Juan, at La Belleza and said, "One thousand dollars," believing they could never begin to possess such a sum. When Juan handed him the money, the man was so struck that he made out a bill of sale. Juan Sanchez and his wife had their home in the Sierra.

When Juan saw the cabin close up, he knew the man had stolen their money. It was small, the roof slanted to one side, the door would not close evenly. The cabin was gradually falling downhill. But it was theirs and he could, with work, repair it. Hurriedly they drove back to Jackson, rented a truck, bought some cheap furniture and hauled it back to the cabin. When they had moved in, Juan brought forth a bottle of whiskey and for the first time in his life proceeded to get truly drunk.

Juan was very happy with La Belleza. She accepted his philosophy completely, understood his need, made it her own. In spite of the people of the town, they created a peculiar kind of joy. And anyway Juan had knowledge about the people.

Twin Pines had been founded, he learned, by one Benjamin Carter, who lived with his daughter in a magnificent house on the hill overlooking town. This Benjamin Carter was a very wealthy man. He had come to the mountains thirty years before to save his marriage, for he had been poor once and loved when he was poor, but then he grew very rich because of oil discovered on his father's Ohio farm and he went away to the city and became incapable of love in the pursuit of money and power. When he at last married the woman whom he had loved, a barrier had grown between them, for Ben Carter had changed but the woman had not. Then the woman became ill and Ben Carter promised her he would take her West, all the way West away from the city so that it could be as it had been in the beginning of their love. But the woman was with child. And so Ben Carter rushed to the California mountains, bought a thousand acres of land, and hurried to build his house before the rain and snows came. He hired many men and the house was completed, except for the interior work and the furnishings. All that winter men he had hired worked in the snow to finish the house while Ben Carter waited with his wife in the city. When it was early spring they set out for California, Ben Carter, his wife, and the doctor, who strongly advised against the rough train trip and the still rougher climb by horse and wagon from Jackson to the house.

But the woman wanted the child born properly, so they went. The baby came the evening of their arrival at the house, and the woman died all night having it. It was this Ben Carter who lived with that daughter now in the great house on the hill, possessing her to the point, it was said about his madness, that he had murdered a young man who had shown interest in her.

Juan learned all this from a Mexican servant who had worked at the great house from the beginning, and when he told the story to La Belleza she wept because of its sadness. It was a tragedy of love, she explained, and Juan—soaring to the heights of his imagination—believed that the town, all one hundred souls, had somehow been infected with the tragedy, as they were touched by the shadow of the house itself, which crept directly up the highway each night when the sun set. This was why they left dead chickens and fish on the porch of the cabin or dumped garbage into the yard. He believed he understood something profound and so did nothing about these incidents, which, after all, might have been the pranks of boys. He did not want the infection to touch him, nor the deeper infection of their prejudice because he was Mexican. He was not indifferent. He was simply too much in love with La Belleza and the Sierra Nevada. Finally the incidents stopped.

Now the life of Juan Sanchez entered its most beautiful time. When the first snows fell he became delirious, running through the pines, shouting, rolling on the ground, catching the flakes in his open mouth, bringing them in his cupped hands to rub in the hair of La Belleza, who stood in the doorway of their cabin laughing at him. He danced, made up a song about snowflakes falling on a desert and then a prayer which he addressed to the Virgin of Snowflakes. That night while the snow fluttered like wings against the bedroom window, he celebrated the coming of the whiteness with La Belleza.

He understood that first year in the mountains that love was an enlargement of himself, that it enabled him to be somehow more than he had ever been before, as though cer-

tain pores of his senses had only just been opened. Whereas
before he had desired the Sierra Nevada for its beauty and
contrast to his harsh fatherland, now he came to acquire a
love for it, and he loved it as he loved La Belleza; he loved it
as a woman. Also in that year he came to realize that there
was a fear or dread about such love. It was more a feeling than
anything else, something which reached thought now and
then, particularly in those last moments before sleep. It was
an absolutely minor thing. The primary knowledge was of the
manner in which this love seemed to assimilate everything,
rejecting all that would not yield. This love was a kind of
blindness.

That summer Juan left La Belleza at times to pick the crops
of the San Joaquin Valley. He had become good friends with
the servant of the big house and this man had access to the
owner's car, which he always drove down the mountain in a
reckless but confident manner. After that summer Juan
planned also to buy a car, not out of material desire, but simply because he believed this man would one day kill himself,
and also because he did not wish to be dependent.

He worked in the walnuts near the town of Linden and
again in the tomatoes of the rich delta. He wanted very much
to have La Belleza with him, but that would have meant more
money and a hotel room in the skidrow, and that was impossible because of the pimps and whores, the drunks and crimi-
nals and the general despair, which the police always tapped
at periodic intervals, as one does a vat of fermenting wine.
The skidrow was a place his love could not assimilate, but he
could not ignore it because so many of his people were lost
there. He stayed in the labor camps, which were also bad because of what the men did with themselves, but they were tol-
erable. He worked hard and as often as he could and gazed at
the mountains, which he could always see clearly in the morning light. When tomato season was over he returned to La
Belleza.

Though the town would never accept them as equals, it
came that summer to tolerate their presence. La Belleza made
straw baskets which she sold to the townspeople and which

were desired for their beauty and intricacy of design. Juan carved animals, a skill he had acquired from his father, and these were also sold. The activity succeeded so well that Juan took a box of their things to Jackson, where they were readily purchased. The following spring he was able to buy the Ford.

Juan acquired another understanding that second year in the mountains. It was, he believed, that love, his love, was the single greatness of which he was capable, the thing which ennobled him and gave him honor. Love, he became convinced, was his only ability, the one success he had accomplished in a world of insignificance. It was a simple thing, after all, made so painfully simple each time he went to the valley to work with face toward the ground, every time he saw the men in the fields and listened to their talk and watched them drive off to the skidrow at night. After he had acquired this knowledge, the nights he had to spend away from La Belleza were occupied by a new kind of loneliness, as though a part of his body had been separated from the whole. He began also to understand something more of the fear or dread that seemed to trail behind love.

It happened late in the sixth year of their marriage. It was impossible, of course, and he spent many hours at the fire in their cabin telling La Belleza of the impossibility, for the doctor had assured him that all had been well tied. He had conducted himself on the basis of that assumption. But doctors can be wrong. Doctors can make mistakes. La Belleza was with child.

For the first five months the pregnancy was not difficult, and he came almost to believe that indeed the passage of La Belleza would open. He prayed to God. He prayed to the earth and sky. He prayed to the soul of his mother. But after the fifth month the true sickness began and he discarded prayer completely in favor of blasphemy. There was no God and never could be God in the face of such sickness, such unbelievable human sickness. Even when he had her removed to the hospital in Stockton, the doctors could not stop it, but it continued so terribly that he believed that La Belleza carried sickness itself in her womb.

After seven months the doctors decided to take the child. They brought La Belleza into a room with lights and instruments. They worked on her for a long time and she died there under the lights with the doctors cursing and perspiring above the large wound of her pain. They did not tell him of the child, which they had cleaned and placed in an incubator, until the next day. That night he sat in the Ford and tried to see it all, but he could only remember the eyes of La Belleza in the vortex of pain. They were of an almost eerie calmness. They had possessed calmness, as one possesses the truth. Toward morning he slumped sideways on the seat and went to sleep.

So he put her body away in the red earth of the town cemetery beyond the cabin. The pines came together overhead and in the heat of midday a shadow sprinkled with spires of light lay upon the ground so that the earth was cool and clean to smell. He did not even think of taking her back to Mexico, since, from the very beginning, she had always been part of that dream he had dreamed. Now she would always be in the Sierra Nevada, with the orange and blue flowers, the quiet deep whiteness of winter, and all that he ever was or could be was with her.

But he did not think these last thoughts then, as he did now. He had simply performed them out of instinct for their necessity, as he had performed the years of labor while waiting for the infant Jesus to grow to manhood. Jesus. Why had he named the boy Jesus? That, perhaps, had been instinct too. He had stayed after La Belleza's death for the boy, to be with him until manhood, to show him the loveliness of the Sierra Nevada, to instruct him toward true manhood. But Jesus. Ah, Jesus. Jesus the American. Jesus of the Flotill. Jesus understood nothing. Jesus, he believed, was forever lost to knowledge. That day with Jesus had been his own liberation.

For a truth had come upon him after the years of waiting, the ultimate truth that he understood only because La Belleza had passed through his life. Love was beauty, La Belleza and the Sierra Nevada, a kind of created or made thing. But there was another kind of love, a very profound, embracing love that he had felt of late blowing across the mountains from the south and that, he knew now, had always been there from the beginning of his life, disguised in the sun and wind. In this love there was blood and earth and, yes, even God, some kind of god, at least the power of a god. This love wanted him for its own. He understood it, that it had permitted him to have La Belleza and that without it there could have been no Belleza.

Juan placed an arm over his eyes and turned to face the wall. The old bed sighed. An image went off in his head and he remembered vividly the lovely body of La Belleza. In that instant the sound that loving had produced with the bed was alive in him like a forgotten melody, and his body seemed to swell and press against the ceiling. It was particularly cruel because it was so sudden, so intense, and came from so deep within him that he knew it must all still be alive somewhere, and that was the cruelest part of all. He wept softly and held the arm across his eyes.

In the dark morning the people of the town were awakened by the blaze of fire that was the house of Juan Sanchez. Believing that he had perished in the flames, several of the townspeople placed a marker next to the grave of his wife with his name on it. But, of course, on that score they were mistaken. Juan Sanchez had simply gone home.

Teacher

There was an English teacher who lived alone in the small upstairs apartment above Miller's garage. After school each day he slowly climbed the wooden steps that led to the tiny rooms, his worn briefcase in his hand, opened the door (it was never locked—who would want to steal what he owned?), and padded to the single bedroom to remove his clothes. Always, on these lengthening days, hot days that crawled like snails toward summer, he returned from school full of oil and sweat, the underarms of his shirt exuding a pale, musty odor, like dead geraniums. Beside himself with discomfort, he performed the ritual of a long hot bath, his fat white body filling the porcelain tub like sausage. The water pounded from the faucet, crept over his legs as he lay there, made a high, round island of his stomach, and then covered it with a wispy swirl of drowning gray hair. He turned the handles with his feet and rested quietly in the water for twenty minutes, a tired old man in the afternoon.

Later, clean and scented, he sat near the front window, a glass of iced tea in his hand and a bowl of Ritz crackers and cheese on the small stand beside him, and waited for the street to come to life. He read or corrected themes, filling the lined pages with red circles, terse abbreviations, and harsh, angry arrows that struck misplaced modifiers and dangling participles with olympian scorn. The sun fell across the blue sky, the children came out to play, erupting up and down the street, and the boys from the high school ground their violent engines about the neighborhood, hunting for girls. At six the noise disappeared and he walked over to the smorgasbord for dinner. When he returned an hour later, he watched television until ten and went to bed, praying he would not waken in the morning dark. One day after the smorgasbord he was startled to find a boy sitting on the narrow steps.

" 'Lo, Mr. Sexton," the boy said, standing. He had enormous blue eyes set deep into a pink, healthy face, a full lower lip, like a girl's, and straw-colored hair. His smooth brow was wrinkled by a frown.

"George," the old man said, "what's wrong?"

The boy shook his head quickly and the hair flopped about, shining in the failing light.

"Stand still, George," the teacher said. "What is it now?"

"I—I wanted to talk to you, Mr. Sexton."

"You're shaking, George," he said. "Is anything wrong?"

The boy tried to hold himself very still, but this only resulted in more severe shaking.

The old man was embarrassed. His face reddened and he put a hand to his mouth, a gesture that had become second nature since he got his false teeth.

"Here, now," he said, "are you hurt? Do you want me to call your parents?"

"Oh, no, no," the boy pleaded, seizing his arm and then dropping it self-consciously. "I'll talk to you, just to you. Please."

He stared at the boy. How the young face looked like all the other young faces. Over the years there had been hundreds and he could not tell them apart. He only just managed to memorize their names each term before they were gone, submerging into the well of his heart like round, smooth stones.

"Well, now," the old teacher said, "let's see here."

"Please, Mr. Sexton."

The boy's hand came out and brushed the old man's sleeve.

An odd current passed through his arm and he drew back. He weighed over twice as much as the boy and was head and shoulders taller, yet the touch embarrassed him, like a caress.

"I guess you could come up for a bit," he said, "upstairs here, where I live."

George nodded quickly and for a moment the two of them raised their heads and looked at the green wall of the apartment.

They climbed the stairs and the old man opened the door. Inside, the air was sweetly scented, for each night, before leaving for dinner, he sprayed the room with pine freshener. How he hated the stale, burnt smells of spring: ashes in a fireplace, dust along the edges of books, the open pores of unswept furniture, warmed by the passionless sun.

"Would you care for a drink?" the teacher asked. "I have tea. Or you could have ice water. Maybe I have some orange juice from this morning."

The boy shook his head. Now that he was in the forbidden sanctum, there was a menacing, ominous certainty about things, as though he had no more time to use, as though his life were unraveling toward an immutable, obscure end.

The old man was totally unnerved. He moved about the small room, arranging magazines, straightening cushions, brushing the backs of chairs, stacking his papers neatly on the coffee table, picking up the crumbs off the floor.

"So school is almost over for you, George," he said, sitting heavily in his chair. What else was there to say? "What are you going to be doing, after the summer I mean?"

George sat on the edge of the sofa, facing sideways toward him. He held his hands together between his knees. "Well, I guess I'll go to junior college and then sell insurance, like my dad."

"Insurance," Sexton said. "Yes, that would be nice." A pale image arose in his imagination, some kingly ghost in an old play about kings, moaning, "Remember me, remember me," and then dying away in the sullen fog beyond the castle wall. How they had murdered *him* over the years with their smooth-faced, impenitent silence, making of him a pale,

striding specter who haunted classroom after classroom, year
after year, in a cheerless longing for sleep.

The young man wrung his hands. "Mr. Sexton," he said.
The teacher turned his watery eyes toward him.

"Mr. Sexton, I'm in trouble, I'm in terrible trouble."

"All right, George," he said.

"I wanted to ask you," George said. "You talk about all
that grammar stuff and you know about where to put all
those marks and how to write things and you know all those
stories and what they mean. You know all that kinda stuff. I
can't figure any of it out, but you know. Gosh, you know all
that stuff, see? You have to be smart to know all that. And I
can't ask my folks or tell my friends or anything like that. I'm
scared, Mr. Sexton, I'm scared."

George began to cry. It was not easy crying, but harsh, bit-
ter, helpless crying. The old man looked away and covered his
mouth with his hand. The room seemed to grow even small-
er, pressing the air from his lungs. Then, after awhile, George
was quiet.

"You know Marla," the boy said, "in my literature class?
She sits next to me in the back row."

The picture of a slim, long-haired girl, a plain-faced girl,
came to his mind and he nodded.

"We've been going together," George said, "and, anyway"
—his lips trembled and bubbles of water appeared in his eyes
—"well, she's my girl friend and now she's pregnant. I'm
scared, Mr. Sexton, I'm real scared." The boy bent toward
him, full of pleading and confusion.

The teacher stood and moved about the room. He wanted
to flee down the steps into the cool night. The confession,
like a wave of thick hot air, was drowning him.

"Mr. Sexton," the boy said.

"George," he said.

"Mr. Sexton, I don't know what to do."

"George, I'm sorry," the old man said. He felt like a dwarf.

"What do I do?" the boy sobbed. "What do Marla and I
do? Our folks will kill us."

"George," he said again. The name hung in his head like a

sign blowing in the wind, like the name of a place, but there were no directions about how to get there, not even an arrow pointing the way.

"I—I know you can't tell me what to do. I know that. I just thought you could say something, that's all. I wanted Marla to come but she was too embarrassed. Mr. Sexton?"

"George," he said.

"What should I do?"

The old man stood facing the window. Outside, the grey light was turning to black. The street lamps were on. He tried to focus his mind and realized he was frightened too.

"I—I can't say," he said.

The boy stood. The old man felt him come up behind him.

"Mr. Sexton, the kids kinda laugh at you a lot, you know. They do their homework in your class. But I always thought you knew a lot. You talk about all those grammar things and all those writers and all." The boy came closer. The old man could hardly breathe. "Gee, I'm scared," George said.

"Tomorrow," the teacher said after a pause. "Come and see me tomorrow."

The boy stepped around him. "You mean at school?"

The old man nodded. "Let me think," he said, "let me think. I can't say anything now."

George nodded. "Think," he repeated. "Yeah, think."

"I'll think," said the old man.

"Gee, thanks, Mr. Sexton, thanks a lot."

"Good night, George," he said.

"Well, good night." The boy went to the door, opened it, and backed slowly out.

The old man stood facing the window. He saw George go down the steps and then cross the street to his car. The car roared to life and sped away. He sat down in the chair to think.

He slept little that night and met the dawn awake and frightened, as far away from the boy as winter from spring. He finished his breakfast of dry cereal and milk and went to school. The English faculty were seated at their desks in the small department office, getting ready for class.

"Hey, what's happening, Papa Sex?" Dick Barkley, the modish department head, laughed. Barkley was forty and dressed like one of the kids. Being relevant, he called it.

"Good morning," he returned, setting his briefcase on his desk and picking up his coffee cup. He filled it at the pot and then sat down. He turned his back to the room, which was an unwritten signal that he wanted to work. He sipped his coffee and tried to think.

George and Marla were in his second class and neither of them appeared. He sighed. Maybe they had just decided and that was that, but when the bell rang he found George waiting for him outside the classroom door.

" 'Lo, Mr. Sexton," he said.

"George."

"Sorry about class. Marla was pretty upset so we decided to cut. She's in the parking lot waiting for me. Did you think of anything."

The teacher looked down at the boy, whose lonely, helpless face made him seem older. "No," he said, "I haven't. I wish I could tell you something. There aren't too many choices and I know you've thought of them all. I'm sorry."

The boy nodded and stared at his feet. "I guess we'll just have to tell our folks and then go from there." He looked up. "Mr. Sexton?"

"Yes, George."

"I've thought of something terrible, you know." A wild glance came to the boy's eyes. "It might hurt Marla. I wouldn't want to hurt Marla."

The old man felt a peculiar compulsion. He raised his arm and found his hand resting on the boy's shoulder. "George," he said, and drops of perspiration stood out on his forehead. "George, why don't you and Marla come to the smorgie tonight with me for dinner?"

"Go to dinner with you?"

"Yes, let me treat you. I want to very much. Then I'll tell you something. Maybe then I can tell you something." The palms of the old man's hands were damp.

"Okay," George said.

"You think it will be all right? Your folks won't mind?"

"No," George said.

"Fine, then, fine. Come to my place at six."

"Okay," George said.

"Okay," said the old man, showing his teeth.

The boy walked away.

The rest of the day passed quickly. He felt light-headed and apprehensive at the same time. He was being moved forward, almost in spite of himself, as though the waters had stirred deep within him and lifted him to the crest of a curling wave. When he got to the tiny apartment that afternoon, he busied himself cleaning the small rooms and dusting the furniture. Somehow everything had to be right, but he wasn't quite sure for what. Then he bathed and shaved again and sat down in his chair next to the window to wait.

At six George arrived alone.

"Marla couldn't come," the boy said.

"You mean she didn't want to."

"Yeah," the boy nodded. "She gets more scared all the time and I don't know what to tell her."

"I understand," the old man said. They stood in the silence for a moment. "Well, let's go to the smorgie."

They went to eat. George filled his plate three times and then had two helpings of dessert. He drank two glasses of milk. The old man smiled.

"I—I haven't had this much to eat for awhile," George said.

"Eat all you want," the old man said, warmed by the boy's vigor.

"Mom, she's been pretty sick lately. And Pop, well, he doesn't pay too much attention."

"I understand," said the old man.

"Mr. Sexton," George said, "why is it people who live together so long can get to be so lousy with each other?"

The old man reddened. "I don't know," he said. "I guess lives have a hard"—he choked a little, swallowed from the glass of water—"well, a hard time living together." He sat forward in the booth. "George, I want to tell you something

—about myself."

"You do?"

"Yes, but not here. You finish up and we'll go back to my place and then I'll tell you. I'll tell you everything you want to know."

The boy cocked his head at the old man and finished his dessert.

Back in the apartment the teacher sat down in the chair by the window and George sat on the sofa. The old man put his hands together.

"George?"

"Yessir."

"I was married, you know. I was married twice." His eyes lifted and turned about the room, half expecting that the cramped silence would echo him and give him reassurance. It only lay back against the walls in mute indifference. "I was married twice in fact," he said.

The boy turned his head a little and regarded him curiously.

"I want to tell you about my first wife. Her name was Meredith and she was beautiful, George, truly beautiful. She was pregnant when we were married." He stopped himself. Pictures of her formed in his brain—slender, dark haired, the hair long and curled about the shoulders. "George, I tried to love her correctly. Well, that's a manner of speaking, you see." He looked at the boy. The smooth, shining face looked back like a stone at the bottom of a pond. The images began to spin in his mind and he remembered everything, all of it, the years and faces and joys and agonies, he remembered what he had tried to forget. "I worshiped her, George. You understand that word worship?"

The boy nodded. "Yessir, I think so."

The old man put his head in his hand. "And then one day there was somebody else."

The boy wiped his mouth and swallowed. He was so embarrassed that his shirt began to grow damp under the arms.

"I cried in my wife's arms. 'You've killed me,' I said, 'you've killed me.' And then I went out and fired a bullet through the window of the man's home. You see, I wanted to fight him, to hurt him, but I knew that was nonsense. I just felt guilty about my wife."

"Yessir," the boy said.

"Well, then it was like a sheet of glass was between us. I could see her, but everything was cold and empty. Then we separated and it was over. Six months after the divorce I married Janet."

He raised his head and looked at the boy. George's eyes were distant and strange and old again.

"I brought her presents," the teacher said. "I gave her gifts. I took her places. We traveled and went to concerts. We did so many things." He paused and lowered his head again. "But she died and I never loved her. I just felt guilty about my first wife." He cried softly, his great shoulders rolling and turning. "You see, I never loved my first wife either. And I don't know why. I don't know why."

"Gee, Mr. Sexton," George said, staring at him.

The old man lifted his red, watery eyes and looked deep into the boy's. "Life happens. There isn't any right or wrong of it. We just have to decide what to do, that's all. I've been afraid a long time, and so I do the same thing over and over again. And here I am, George."

"Gee," the boy said.

"And that's all I can tell you, George, that's all I have to tell."

They both sat very still for a long time, and he looked at the boy and the boy looked at him and at that moment there just wasn't any life anywhere else in the world, and a terrible thing moved inside him.

"I'm sorry, Mr. Sexton."

The old man nodded. "A long time ago," he said, "a long time."

George stood up. "I guess we'll get married," he said. "I mean we talked it over and we decided, even before I came here tonight, Mr. Sexton. We're gonna get married." The boy's voice was flat and even.

"Oh, George," the old man said.

"We'll do that," he said. "There's the operation, you know, the abortion? But, well—" The boy's eyes flared to life again. "Mr. Sexton, I don't wanna get married. I don't." They stood there a moment and George put out his hand. "Thanks for the dinner," he said.

The old man nodded. They rose and he opened the door. George stepped through and turned about. He looked at the boy. He knew him. He knew him as well as he knew himself. They were the same, boy and old man. They shared fate helplessly, like things preyed upon beneath the sea. George would marry the girl and sell insurance and find oblivion in policies and premiums, and he would fail a few more years, haunt a few more classrooms, and then disappear into the sullen fog. It all came down to this, this lonely bottom of the heart. And in the dry place, the place of stone, there was no hope or joy, no beginning, but only the passionless emptying of life and the understanding. Obscure ends and tombstones tilted in the summer grass.

Then he became angry. The anger flickered up from the ashes of his despair. Over the years he had pitied himself and hidden from himself, but now the anger burned and lit the darkness of his heart. He understood that all he had ever had to offer was his own story, but instead he had given punctuation and grammar and disguised himself from the world; and, except for the boy, he was still disguising himself, still hiding. The anger, lighting the waste and emptiness, became a terrible thing within him, but it gave him back what he had lost.

"Love, George," he said.

"What?" the boy said, standing in the dark beyond the threshold.

The old man reached out and pulled him back into the light. "I'll pay for it or whatever. Whatever it takes, I'll take care of it."

"Mr. Sexton?" George said.

"George, kill the child," the teacher said. "Kill the child."

The boy stared at him in mute affirmation.

The Old Maid

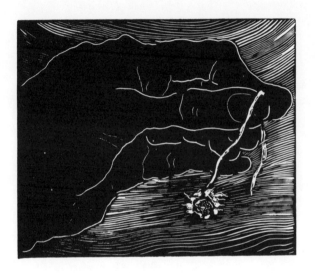

Beyond the office windows the autumn day possessed an intense clarity, the way white wine looks through a green bottle. Yes, she liked that image and made a note of it on the scratch pad she always kept on her desk. It was as though the sky was getting ready to pour forth a clearer, brighter liquid. She imagined it spilling over the library building across the way and over the oaks on the west lawn and farther, over the trees at Swenson Park, where the students smoked cigarettes and lounged on the uncut grass. And, perhaps, just for a moment, a kind of wet, tinsel light did appear, like a suddenly visible wind, and fall over all the life outside. It certainly seemed so, and the sensation made her blush with embarrassment. She placed a hand against her face and noticed that Glenn Barton, the divorced senior English teacher, was watching her again and smiling. That embarrassed her even more and she grew suddenly angry at him. For two years he had looked at her like that, as if he knew the color of her thoughts, and she almost couldn't bear it. But what was she to do, except let him see her anger? She dared not hate him. She feared the hatred within her the way one fears a cancer. And so she was only angry at him, almost always, it seemed, and called him by his last name.

"Hey, Barton," she would say when he was singing (he was always singing, and, maddeningly, he had a lovely voice), "what's that one? I never heard that one before either."

"That's too bad," he would laugh (he had a deep, beautiful laugh and that made her angry too). "You've had a deprived childhood."

"You're just too old," she would return (it had taken her a year and a half to get the courage to say this to him. He was at least forty, she was certain, with warm streaks of white at the temples of his black hair).

"You're just too young," he would come back, laughing that laugh of his.

She would turn away from him, pulling her sweater across her shoulders, and be angry. One thing that did, though. It made her skin white again so he could not see inside her.

But minutes later he would walk by her desk, pat her head and say, "It is a beautiful day, isn't it, Kat?" And her face would flame with a deeper burning. She couldn't speak to him for days after that, and all the sky and grass and wind could burst apart outside for all she might notice, so busy was she with the terrible secret of herself.

She was in love.

Kathryn Morgan opened her purse and removed the pocket compact. The oval mirror appeared and there was the face.

It was plain. She was a plain-faced woman (from a distance her face seemed attractive enough, particularly in soft light — she often stood far back and looked at her reflection that way — but when you got close, you saw that the nose was too broad, the lips too full, and there was a tiny mole growing on her left cheek). She was thick looking, almost stout, but not fat. She had long blonde hair, which she drew down severely over her ears and fastened behind the head with a white bone clip. She wore plain-colored blouses with tiny floral print skirts (one of the flowers of which always matched the blouse) and crepe-soled shoes. In the winter she wore heavy white sweaters — always white — and clean wool pants.

She drove a yellow Opel Kadet with an f.m. radio and lived alone in a one bedroom apartment in Colonial Estates. At night she cooked things like Teriyaki steak with natural rice and later sipped Earl Grey tea while she corrected themes. In the morning she carried a sack lunch to school in a black Samsonite case, along with a small jar of freeze-dried coffee and tiny packages of powdered milk she stole from the Denny's where she ate on the weekends.

She was plain, simply and directly plain, and she reiterated that judgment in the mirror again this morning, as she had every morning as far back as she could remember. She knew and accepted the inevitability of truth. She had entered teaching, after an uneventful college career, pale-faced, empty of inspiration, dull, plodding even (she knew her imagination was not quick, that things often "surprised" her) and now, three years later and twenty-five, her life had assumed the patterns she relied upon for survival. Indeed, she always seemed to be waiting in another universe for a creator who never appeared. She did not even understand why she had chosen teaching to spend her time in, except that it was something so opposite to what her overbearing, narrow-minded father had done and so out of character for her docile, submissive, housewife of a mother. "Get married and let a man take care of you," she had said. "Why do you want a career of your own?" Her sister Anne, who did get married, said that at least teaching was something you could always fall back on.

So she had fallen.

And there it was. No lived life, no felt heart, no diamonds or rubies, only dry sand stones in a dry desert, and days and days and days. Life was an answer to which she had been the wrong question.

But something had happened, something totally unexpected and unplanned for. She liked teaching. She actually and truly liked it. It surprised her, amazed her. That first year had been difficult, of course (more so for her, it seemed, pushed as she was by a burdensome sense of duty) but she actually and truly enjoyed being with the students, particularly the boys. Strange, unexpected sensations passed through her when she was with the boys. They would come into her office after class, maybe three or four, with questions and awkward smiles (they elbowed each other when they thought she wasn't looking or winked at each other—she was obviously having an effect upon them, and this pleased her). They sat on the edge of the desk or knelt before her on the carpet to talk, and she burned with a slow burning.

She did not understand this feeling, of course, and it embarrassed her in the way that Glenn Barton embarrassed her, yet it was all right. With the boys it was all right because it was so webby and gave her a kind of pleasure, the kind one has when watching someone unobserved, and she watched the boys and felt warm and vulnerable and it was all right, the embarrassment, it was pleasurable. Yes, she liked it.

Sometimes, leaning over the green blotter on her desk to talk to a boy, she would shake her head and a strand of hair would come loose from the bone clip and float above her face, rising and falling as she breathed, and she didn't notice. Her voice never seemed to lift with excited expression, even when she was angry (she was angry at the students too, of course, but it was always all right. She never held any grudges for laziness). Instead it fell at the end of sentences as though the weight of words was too much for her lips to carry. The boys, by contrast, had voices that jumped and chirruped about her, like monkeys in a cage.

The flesh of her arms and face was a mottled white, suffused under the surface by a kind of watery red, as though the veins had been stretched and bled thinly and unevenly. When she was embarrassed, these slender vines would tear and her skin would flush.

At first she did not understand. She believed it was that the boys were so young and yet so close to her own age (after all, twenty-five was only eight years away from Tommy Wegman, who was seventeen—her sister had married a man ten years older than she). Being so near to and yet so above them (she was, of course, an adult) she felt a kind of permission, a kind of yielding of herself she had never before experienced. This realization caused her the acutest embarrassment, for she wondered if she were unhealthy or misshapen in some way. How could boys make a grown woman feel so vulnerable? But they did, and she tried to hide the peculiarity of it by paying attention to all her students equally.

But the girls did not come around much. If they did, it was

to obtain page numbers or reference books or to ask for information. Only the boys visited. Because, try as she might, she only wanted the boys to visit, and they would leave her, feeling slightly confused, as though they had been told something they could just faintly not hear. That had been the first year. In the second she had decided to narrow her attention to a few boys. She would encourage only a few to linger in the office after the bell, while enjoying all the others from a kind of high place behind her desk in the classroom. But, at the end of the second year, she knew even that was not enough. The focus was too blurred, the intensity was too diffuse. And then this term had come around, her third year of teaching, and there was Tommy Wegman, a gentle, quiet, brown-haired boy in her fifth class, who had read Goethe already and Tolstoy, two of her diamonds of lived life, and she stopped struggling against the inevitability of herself.

Because she knew at last what it was. It was the passion breaking just beneath her skin, it was her own passion, her own living life. She blushed it back when Tommy came to see her that first time, just as she had with all the other boys, but the flash of his warm, dark eyes humbled her. She shot a quick, toothless smile across her face and then withdrew beneath her skin, but the passion trembled there, breaking the blood in her body and sending it to the surface. It was the summary of her unmet heart, the thing to which the strands of feeling over the years had been tied, the center of herself, the nucleus of her fear to be. She let herself feel the possibility of it. She toyed with the imagination of it, she lingered in the reality of her undoing. She loved Tommy Wegman. She loved him. She nurtured it and tended it with fantasy and daydream. She swam in the luxury of a free heart and planned to be with him, worked to be with him. And tonight, this very night, he was coming to her tiny apartment to get extra help on his grammar skills. And she would have things to eat and things to drink and the living room would bathe in flowers and soft light. And, after all, she could be the right question to life, there could be a second coming.

"Lovely to be alive, isn't it, Kat?" Glenn Barton said,

touching her shoulder as he passed by her desk to his next class, and she put her head down on her arms.

The small living room floated in a warm yellow light. On the bookcase against the far wall a single bayberry candle burned, giving off a scent of crushed green leaves. On the coffee table before the couch she had placed small China bowls filled with Jordan almonds and chocolate peanuts (she was sure he would like one of these and Jordan almonds were her favorite). The thick, Spanish-looking dining room table gleamed like oil, and a fresh bouquet of carnations stood in the exact corner on a paper doily (she had bought them that afternoon, since there was absolutely nowhere in this tiny place where she could grow flowers). In the kitchen the water for tea was ready and she had coffee crystals in case he wanted coffee. Of course, she had milk and Pepsi and some Hershey's cocoa. She had even bought a few pastries, an eclair, a pop-over, two plain glazed doughnuts. She couldn't think of anything else. There wasn't anything else to do. At six-thirty she put on her new pale blue blouse with the matching gray and blue print skirt and sat down to wait. He came at seven-ten.

Tommy Wegman was a tall, slender boy with light brown hair and deep brown eyes. His face was square and the expression open and guileless, as though he had just come out into the sunlight from an afternoon matinee. He wore a dark blue cardigan over a white tee shirt and faded blue jeans. He looked to her almost like something he could never be, an innocent young boy in the spring of life. He was carrying his three-hole binder and his *Warriner's*.

" 'Lo, Miss Morgan," he said. His voice was too deep for such a shy face.

"Hello, Tommy," she said. "Well, come in, come in."

"Okay," he said, ducking his head, "sure."

He stepped over the threshold and looked about, waiting for her to tell him what to do next.

"You brought your things," she said.

"Yes, my essays, all the ones you passed back."

"Well, that's a good idea."

"You can show me what I did."

She clasped her hands together. "Well, may I get you anything to drink? I have cocoa, milk, coffee, tea—"

"Cocoa's fine."

"I have Pepsi too."

"Cocoa's fine."

"All right. Why don't you just make yourself to home and I'll fix it. Have some things there on the table."

He looked at the China bowls.

"I'll have a little surprise for you later, some things I got at the bakery."

He blushed. "Gee, Miss Morgan—"

"It's nothing," she said, "absolutely nothing. I loved doing it, honesty I did. I don't have too many people over—." She felt momentarily confused and wanted to explain her entire life to him. Instead she stopped and stared at him. His clear brown eyes were unbearable. "Just sit down there, Tommy, and help yourself. I'll be right back."

She turned the corner into the small kitchen and leaned up against the refrigerator. She rested her face against the cool, white door and took several deep breaths. Then she put on the teapot of water for the cocoa.

When it was done, she brought the two cups into the living room and set one before him. She saw he had eaten some of the peanuts and that pleased her.

He smiled. "It has marshmallows," he said.

"Oh, is that all right?" she asked.

"I like marshmallows in my cocoa."

"So do I."

"They get all soft and sweet."

"I know," she breathed.

She reached for her cup at the same time he did. His hand brushed against her fingers and she felt thin wisps of air move down the back of her neck. They picked up their cups and sipped the hot liquid.

"You've got a chocolate mustache," she said, laughing.

"So do you," he grinned.

She wanted to take the tip of her finger and touch the brown line above his lip. She wondered if it would taste like her own. He positioned himself on the couch and she felt the shy movement of him reach her through the cushion, like a cottony wave. A queer little silence crept under the door and lay down at their feet.

"Well," she said at last, "now let's look at those essays."

"Okay," he said.

He opened the binder and took out three papers. They were arranged in the chronological order in which she had assigned them.

They worked for about forty-five minutes. He seemed to have particular trouble with introductory groups of words, nominative absolutes and adverbial clauses. There was some difficulty with the use of internal commas and he had no conception at all of a semicolon. He was mixed up about *lie* and *lay, sit* and *set, rise* and *raise*. Sometimes, compositionally, he tended to get carried away with his own personal flights of fancy and leave the topic at hand. But that was understandable. He should try out his wings, and she already knew she was going to recommend him for Barton's creative writing class next year. All this was good for her and calmed her somewhat, though each time the edges of their skin touched or even the fabric of their clothes as they leaned close together, studying the words on the page, tiny ripples of feeling would pass through her body, like stones dropped into a quiet, clear pool. He finished the bowl of chocolate nuts but didn't touch one Jordan almond.

"My, that's enough," she declared finally. "We've been working hard."

He sat back, a slightly dazed look on his face.

"It wasn't too much, was it, Tommy?"

"Oh, no, no, Miss Morgan. There's just a lot to writing well, I guess."

"You write very well, Tommy. You know you do. These are just tools. They either use you or you use them. Knowing how to use them, you'll write better."

"Thanks," he said. "Thanks a lot."

She looked at his eyes. In the deep, clear irises she could see the reflection of herself, tiny Kathryns shining more brightly and more brilliantly than the Kathryn of real life. She wondered if he saw the face she saw in his eyes or if he looked right through to her pale, plain actuality. And surely he was mirrored in her eyes. Did he see himself there, brilliant and beautiful, the same in both realities? Did he know what he was to her?

He looked away, and a redness crept into his cheeks. She trembled. Had she inadvertently told him something? Was she too obvious? Did he know she loved him?

Loved him.

Tommy Wegman felt as though someone else were in the room watching them. That was the only way he could explain the strange feeling that had come over him. It was a little like getting home too late at night and expecting his father to be awake waiting for him.

"Is anything wrong, Tommy?" she asked.

"No, Miss Morgan."

Something wavering hung in the air, something red and tentative. Her terrible fear was held only just at bay by the half-yielding of herself to an adolescent with blemishes at the corners of his mouth. She leaned toward him ever so slightly, as though a wind had touched her.

"You have such a creative mind, Tommy," she said. "You're so creative."

"Thank you," he said looking down at the soft pastel colors of the candied almonds.

"It's a gift, a beautiful gift."

He nodded, embarrassed.

"Cherish it always. Oh, don't betray it, Tommy." She raised a hand and the fingers looked for somewhere to go, someplace to touch. He watched them linger before him, like tapered shells.

"I will," he said.

"Tommy," she said.

"Yes, Miss Morgan?"

He looked at her and all her life poised on the invisible

plain that was her minutes and hours and days. The question swelled and lifted, waiting, waiting at her fingertips for the creator of the universe to come out of hiding and answer it with the great roll of his muscled arm. But Tommy picked up his papers and her fingers fell back and lay unmoving on her lap, as though all the life had been let out of them. Nothing had happened.

Nothing, finally, would ever happen.

"Well," he smiled clumsily.

"Yes," she said.

"I want to thank you for everything. It sure was a lot of help and nice of you to let me come to your apartment because I have a job after school and couldn't come then."

"Wouldn't you like a popover, Tommy, or an eclair? That was the surprise. I have some doughnuts too."

"I'd better be going, Miss Morgan. I have some other homework." He stood up awkwardly, as though his legs had gone to sleep.

"Well, I'm glad I could help," she said, standing too. "I want you to take those pastries home with you."

"Oh, I couldn't Miss Morgan—"

"Really, now. I can't eat them myself. You have a little brother, don't you? You can share them."

"Yes'm," he said.

"Good. Now I'll just get a bag to put them in. You take them home."

He nodded. She gathered the pastries, laid them in a brown bag with napkins between them and returned to the living room. "Here, now. *Bon appetit.*"

"Gee, thanks, Miss Morgan."

They walked to the door and she opened it.

"Well, good night, Miss Morgan, and thanks again."

"Good night, Tommy, see you tomorrow."

He stepped away and she closed the door after him. She went to the couch and sat down. She felt anxious and alone. It as as though something were bursting, bursting to get out of or inside her. She couldn't be sure.

She turned off the lights and went into the bedroom. She

took off her clothes, but before she pulled the flannel night-gown over her head, she sat on the edge of the bed and looked down the curve of her body. The breasts were swollen and firm and the nipples stood out like the bruised heels of ripe acorns. She allowed the fingers of that same right hand to move tentatively down between the breasts to the flesh of her stomach. They paused there. She watched the hand. The fingers went ever so slowly and a pulse began to beat beneath her ears. The fingers touched the twisted nest of hair and stopped, trembling. She broke into a sweat and closed her eyes in fear and disbelief. She had seen something reaching up from beneath her, a red, firm finger reaching for the tip of her own trembling touch, and she understood, and her hand hesitated and then limped away like a broken spider.

She sighed heavily and the breath passed through her, blowing out candles and slamming doors. Now she knew what it was about Glenn Barton. She had felt him calling, calling to her, but like a trumpet, sounding clearly from the top of a stone wall in an empty desert. Beneath the anger she had feared him, feared what he could do to her, how he could make her reach down into the red pulse of herself. He was a large, beautiful, made thing. She could not, simply could not leave her little oasis to seek him in Nineveh where he lived.

And Tommy Wegman was responsible for this understanding. He had liberated her. His clumsiness was her triumph. He echoed her own half-felt life, her own feeble self-exposure, the things Glenn had the power to open, like the pages of a book. His awkwardness pierced her flesh and yet no blood flowed. It stayed safe below the surface, bursting in red bloom under the white flesh. Because he could not see. He could not know. Had she wanted him to truly touch her? Had she wanted to touch him, to feel the cool, moist scent of his breath on hers? No! Certainly not! Of course not! Such an idea was repulsive to her now. It was gross, cruel and unbalanced. But hadn't she thought so, hadn't her fantasies regarding him been sensual, erotic, touched with heat and smell? No! No! Never! That was the target for some arrow she could never release. She knew, then, that she loved Tommy Wegman even more, with a different, truer love, and that there would be others, many others just like him.

She would always be young next to them, no matter how old she became. She would always be excited and vulnerable and young next to their youth. She would be the same inside, just like them. She might grow old and even, one day, she might die, but she would always be like them, and their youth, from year to year, would only reflect her true spirit. She would always be a girl for they would always be young boys, and she would smile at them out of a knowledge so private and so perfect that not even the angels could pry it from her. No man would ever take away that shy innocence and render her outside herself. She was too perfect a lover for that.

The Autumn of Henry Simpson

Henry Simpson went often to the park these lonely autumn days. No one else was there. It was cold and the wind blew hard and the storm clouds rolled against the blue sky. The cold wind pulled the branches of the trees and the leaves spun and twisted crazily, trying to hold on, and then fell sideways down the empty air until they covered the ground. Even then the wind would not let them be. In strong gusts it turned the leaves on end, pushed them frantically over the grass or lifted them in droves, like dry paper birds taking flight. They flew under passing cars or smashed against tree trunks and park benches. They covered the walkways, gathered and grew black under the evergreens. Then, after a while, the trees would be empty and the wind would not sound in them like something being dragged across the sky but more like something thin and sharp and hollow. Then the grass would be clean and the streets and walkways would be hard and grey. The leaves would all be gone, like the birds, gathered and burned somewhere by men in yellow raincoats.

He knew what it meant. He knew it in his bones, that were as dry and fragile as the autumn leaves. His hat pulled securely over his bald head, a muffler tightened about his throat, his great, grey overcoat buttoned to the chin and his gloved hands stuffed in his pockets, he walked slowly through the park, punishing himself with melancholy and guilt. What had been done or not done, or what done had not been done properly or enough? What had not been said or what, having been said, was a lie and a sham? Had there been something or someone he could have loved and had not? Could he have become someone who would have known what he did not know? Was there some place in the world where he could have lived more than he had lived? The questions tormented him and made his heart beat fast. What did it all mean? Did it mean anything? Did every man come to this place of sad self-laceration and doubt? The town was filled with old men, but only he walked the park in the sullen afternoons.

It was over for Emily. She lay under the earth, no more than a memory in his mind, all the dryness of her old face gone to ashes and dust. He thought of her like that some- times. She had been dead eight years and sometimes he saw right through the ground and into that coffin with the silver handles, where she slept like a withered ghost. Oh, God, how terrible it was to hang on past someone you had lived with all those years! Echoing rooms, white, unwashed walls, empty geranium pots, sunlight staining a worn carpet, and doors that never opened. All the moments and all the gestures of the years, all the words that had filled those familiar spaces were gone now, leaving only the stark, staring furniture and the smell of loneliness. And the thoughts, like boulders, tumbling and thudding against his heart, breaking the flesh and scattering the blood he had so carefully saved and nur- tured. Why couldn't the mind rest, like the body, and be at peace? He doubted now that he had ever known Emily, much less loved her. There were only photograph albums and cameo rings and porcelain cups and saucers. Sometimes he would go whole days without being able to remember her and what she looked like. It terrified him and made him guilty and ashamed. It seemed so easy to be dead and so hard to be alive that he envied her that solemn silence.

His daughter Margaret came to the house for her weekly visit and said, "You ought to go out more, Dad, make new friends. You shouldn't just sit around.

He looked at her. She was thirty-eight and there were crow's feet at the corners of her eyes and circles around her throat. The flesh was getting loose on her upper arms and her thighs had widened. And he wondered, had he been so fool- ish as to give advice like that to his parents? She wanted him to go forward, to think about tomorrow, when all the while his life was like a museum, where he wandered from room to room trying to guess what the people had been like.

"I'm all right, dear," he said quietly, "really I am."

She gave him a look one reserves for a child who cannot comprehend something perfectly simple. "Well, you ought to get out more."

He lifted his shoulders and felt guilty for not living up to her expectations. That made him angry but he only smiled and said, "Really, dear."

His two grandchildren, Tommy, who was twelve, and Ginger, who was eight, ran about making the house echo strangely. He sighed and she took it as some acquiescence.

"After all," she said, "Mother's been dead a long time now."

"I know," he said.

She looked at him deeply, as if she had said the most profound of things, something that should lift him and make him realize everything as it truly was, something that should change his life — a penetrating look, it was called — but he was only bored with her stupidity. Truly, she was stupid, and he found himself wishing he had had someone else for a daughter, Beverly Long, for example, who lived down the street and always had a cheery "good morning" for him when he walked by. What did someone who had divorced her husband after only seven years of marriage know? And he had always liked Bill, her husband — her ex-husband — he missed Bill. He could talk to Bill. What was Bill doing now? He wondered.

"You can take care of yourself, can't you, Dad?" she said carefully.

And there it was. The Topic. The second, actually, for the first was always Getting Out Of The House And Making New Friends. The first he could endure, but this one frightened him terribly. She never said anything else. She didn't have to. The Topic made the great hole open before his feet, the great dark hole with no bottom. Oh, she wanted to push him into it, she would have loved to push him into it, to find him weak and defenseless and utterly without hope. And then she would have him in one of those homes, where he would lie, toothless and open-mouthed on a white cot, shrinking helplessly into oblivion. Was she really like that, really, or was that only the desperate suspicion of his own confused mind?

"Of course, dear, of course," he said quickly. "I manage fine, wash and cook for myself. Mrs. Fergusson comes in to clean whenever I need her. I'm fine, dear, really." How he hated her!

"Well, you're sure now?" She looked him over, examining him meticulously. He felt naked.

"Of course," he said.

"Well, then, I'll be running along. Children," she called. They scampered into the room and stood beside their mother, regarding him curiously. "Give Papa a kiss goodbye." They fumbled toward him and he offered his cheek. Their lips were thin and wet. Margaret stood up and straightened her dress.

"Goodbye, dear," he said. "Goodbye, Tommy and Ginger. Here's a dollar for each of you."

"Thank you," Ginger said.

"Thank you," said Tommy.

He sat, looking at his grandchildren, wondering what the dollars had bought.

"Well, we'll be running along," his daughter said. "Look in on you next week. Don't get up. It's all right." She moved away, then turned. "Honestly, I worry about you all alone."

"I'm fine, fine," he said, begging with his eyes for her to go. "I watch television. I'm catching up on my reading. Really, dear, I'm fine." Why did he have to reassure her about her own neglect?

"All right, then, goodbye."

He nodded and they were gone.

The house felt like a great, cold stone, sinister and unyielding. He thought about looking at television or reading some back issues of *National Geographic*. He was getting a little hungry. But he just sat, watching the afternoon move into the room. Then he fell asleep.

When he awoke it was dark. It surprised and frightened him that he had slept like that. He got up slowly. His legs were stiff and sore and his back hurt. He turned on all the living room lights and drew the curtains. That was better. He went into the kitchen, soft-boiled two eggs, made some toast in the oven and poured himself a glass of milk. It was good to have something to do and he tried not to look at the backs of his hands. Then he ate, slowly, and that took time too. When he was done, he went back into the living room and sat down.

He knew he should go to bed. He wasn't tired, though. He wasn't even sleepy. But there was nothing he wanted to do. He stayed there a while, holding on to the last few hours of the day. That made him feel ridiculous because he had tried that many times before, and nothing happened. The room stayed the same, filled with orange lamplight and dull, still shadow. The clock ticked over the mantel and the television stared at him with its single opaque, flat green eye. He got up, checked the doors, turned off all the lights and went to bed.

He lay under the covers and looked into the darkness. He seemed to be floating in the darkness. Funny how, even after all these years since Emily's death, he slept on his side of the bed. He did not move to the center or throw his arms out and when he awoke in the morning, there he was, spread down his side of the bed, while the other half was empty, cold and dry.

Habit, he thought, that was all. Everything was habit, was getting used to. A man built his whole life on it, he waited for all the parts of it to occur, he needed for them to occur again and again. It was the pattern, the meaning of things. Habit was life itself. And now he stood outside it all, watching the parts move ever and ever more slowly, like a machine running down.

Then he thought about Emily and all the times they had made love here when they were young, and all the times when Margaret was in school and the times when they were older and then when they were old and only slept night after night together in the quiet dark. All those years of lovemaking and he could not remember just what it had been like or even if it had been love. What a terrible thought! But if it was a time for doubting, then he might as well doubt that too.

He found, as the days and weeks passed, that he had a harder and harder time holding on to anything. That must be what dying was. He didn't know or understand, but it must be like that, just letting go of everything, until you just let go of the last thing and it was all over.

A shudder passed through him. Why was it that life exacted this final penance, why it waited until you had no strength or will? Why did it save the most momentous thing of all for the end? Questions and no answers. Where were the answers? Maybe there were none. No answers? Deliberately and purposely, no answers? He looked into the darkness and saw only that it was dark. He smiled to himself and didn't know why. He had thought about it all before and would think about it all again and again. What he needed was new evidence, new data. He needed to let fresh light into the museum. He lay there, watching the room. Once in a while a car passed by on the street outside. Then, after a long time, he went to sleep.

He got up the following morning and took a hot shower. Then he shaved, dressed and went into the kitchen to make coffee. Every morning he made coffee. There was the smell of it brewing and the sound and the brown color of it sliding down the sides of the tiny glass dome. The little orange light on the top of the handle went "click" when the coffee was done. Then he took a pot holder and lifted out the steaming basket of hot, wet grounds. Emily had always done that. He poured himself a cup, poached two eggs, opened a new can of tomato juice and went into the dining room. He set everything on the table and got the paper from the front porch. Then he sat down.

He drank the tomato juice first. A morning just wasn't a morning without some kind of juice, cold and fresh and enlivening a mouth stale from sleep. Then he quickly ate the eggs and sipped at his coffee while he thumbed through the headlines of the paper. That's all he ever did now, read the headlines. The details of events did not interest him. When Emily was alive, he had read the whole paper, every article, and watched the evening news on television. He had wonderd what things meant and why they happened as they did and how they would affect the nature of the things they affected. He even read the sports page, puzzling over scores, series, rounds, matches, statistics. This morning he could not get halfway through the headlines before he closed the paper and pushed it aside. He sighed, leaned back in the chair and put his fingers around the coffee cup.

After a while the phone rang. It was Margaret. She was coming over, alone. Now what's this all about? he thought, getting up to clear away the breakfast dishes. When he was done in the kitchen, he went to the living room to wait. In a few minutes she arrived.

"Hello, Dad," she said sitting on the sofa beside him.

"What's wrong?" he asked warily.

"Nothing's wrong. Why does something have to be wrong?"

"You don't come over twice in a row like that," he said.

"Oh," she said, embarrassed, and then he wished he hadn't said it.

"Who's minding the grandchildren?" he asked.

"Mrs. Carson."

"She's nice."

"The children simply love her."

He was silent and she looked at her hands, which were gloved. Then he looked at them.

"I was thinking," she said, "why don't you and I just go for a little drive today?"

"A drive?"

"Yes, why not? Just the two of us."

Was she feeling guilty? he thought. "Where would we go?" he asked.

"Oh, just around. The colors are lovely this time of year. C'mon."

"I don't know," he said.

"C'mon, now. It will do you good." She pulled him by the arm.

"Oh, all right," he said.

They stood up and he got his overcoat from the closet. They went out to the car and he climbed in beside her. They drove past the park and then up Pershing to Harding.

"Let's go out to the river," she said. "Remember how we used to go out there when I was little? We'd have a picnic and you'd fish and there'd be all the boats going up and down?"

"I remember," he said.

They drove up on the levee road along Smith Canal and out past Pixie Woods, a children's park and playground. The road curved around by the Rod and Gun Club and then up along the San Joaquin River. There were all the Navy ships from the war in mothballs. They were old and grey and sat sullen and useless on the muddy water. They depressed him terribly.

"Would you like to park and walk down to the water where we used to fish?" she asked.

"No," he said, "no, I wouldn't." Everything looked foreign and strange to him, yet oddly familiar, like a place you've visited only once and then come back to.

"Would you like to stop and look at the boats for a while?" she asked.

"No," he said, "let's go back."

"Are you all right, Dad?"

"Of course, dear, of course," he said, trying to smile. If this was Getting Out Of The House, he hated it.

She turned the car around. "I have one more place I want to stop," she said.

"What is it?" he asked, regarding her suspiciously.

"Just a place I want to see. I think you'll like it."

"They turned down off the river road. "I want to go home," he said.

"Let's just see this place first, Dad. Please."

"I said take me home. I don't want to go anyplace. I don't want to see anyplace."

"We'll go home in a little while, but first I want you to visit this place."

He was frightened. "You tricked me," he said. "You deliberately tricked me into leaving the house. I know where you want to put me. I know. You've been threatening me and now you're doing it."

"Dad."

"I know where you're taking me." His hands were trembling in his lap. "And I won't let you," he said. "Take me home this instant."

She held the steering wheel tightly in both hands. They came back onto Pershing and drove north. "I will," she said. "But I'm going to show you this place. I knew you would never go on your own. But you don't know anything about these rest homes." He shivered at the word. "And neither did I until I did some investigating. Honestly, Dad, it's not good for you to be all alone in that house day after day. You need people your own age to talk to and have fun with. I found a real nice home. The people are marvelous and they have planned activities and everything. You'd always have something to do."

He glared at her and said nothing more.

The place was called Mid-Valley Retirement Home. She stopped the car in the lot. "C'mon, Dad," she said. He remained motionless and she got out and came around to his side of the car and opened the door. "Please, Dad," she said, "don't be difficult. Will you at least come and look?" She pulled at his arm. The best way was to just get it over with, he thought, just humor her and then he'd be home and he'd never trust her again. She was as stubborn as her mother. He got out slowly and they walked to the front steps. He grit his teeth as they passed through the glass doors.

"Wait here, Dad," she said. "I'll find Doctor Mercer."

He stood alone looking about. Immediately to his right was a kind of open room. There was a large color television against the wall. A half dozen people, who looked as old as mountain tops, sat in wheel chairs facing the screen. They turned to look at him with blank, stupified faces. Across the vast chasm of all the years their eyes met like strangers, and yet there was a kind of recognition, a kind of expression that said, "Oh, yes, so you are come here too." Their eyes terrified him. There were some people in bathrobes sitting in stuffed chairs or flowered sofas reading magazines. A woman was shuffling about, her body in one of those light, tubular frames that support your weight. Suddenly he was very conscious of his own body and apprehensive about its adequacy. At that moment Margaret returned with a man dressed in a white garment. He had a moustache and was smiling.

"Dad, this is Doctor Mercer. He's the director of the home."

The man in white thrust out his hand with insolent assurance. "Good day, Mr. Simpson," he said. "I'm so glad you came to visit us. I hope you'll like us and decide to stay with us."

He dropped the man's hand and drew back.

"Dad," Margaret said.

The man in white smiled. "It's understandable," he said. "Often the first reaction is quite surprised. That's only because it's all new. Right, Mr. Simpson?"

"Margaret, I've seen enough," he said. "I want to leave."

"Daddy," she said.

"I want to leave."

They stood there a moment. The old people seemed to float around him, like flotsam thrown up from a sunken ship.

"Look us over, Mr. Simpson," the man said. "Give us a chance."

"C'mon, Dad," Margaret said, pulling his arm.

He began to sweat profusely. His shirt stuck to his back. His face grew hot and then cold. His heart thudded in his chest. The doctor talked about the facility, something about recreation and activities and he could even have his own room, if he liked. Everywhere there were old people, some so old that he thought it impossible they could ever have been children. They walked down a hallway of rooms, the doctor talking and talking, and then they passed one doorway and he looked in.

Lying on a white, narrow bed was the oldest man he had ever seen. His head was deep in the pillow, as though growing there. The face was so thin that the flesh looked painted upon the bones and was stretched from jaw to cheek. The face was covered with whiskers and the toothless mouth was open, forming a hole the size of a small coin. He could hear the breath passing back and forth through this opening, and then the old man turned his skeletal head and regarded him with horrible, watery grey eyes. Henry screamed.

"Dad!" said Margaret.

"Oh, God!" he cried. "Oh, God!" He backed away until he bumped up against the far wall of the corridor. Still his eyes were fixed on the old man's, and the grey eyes were confused and lost and pleading with him. "No," he whispered, "oh, no." He turned his face away. The doctor came to him and put one hand on each shoulder.

"Mr. Simpson," he said.

"Please," he begged, "oh please." Then he pulled away from the doctor, stumbled, then hurried up the hallway.

"Father!" Margaret demanded.

His hat was in his hand, his arms waving, the coat spilling out around him like a parachute that had failed to open. The clap of his feet on the vinyl floor caused the wheelchairs to swivel and magazines to fall and all the old eyes regarded him with shocked surprise. A nurse, carrying a round aluminum tray covered with tiny white paper cups, stepped out of his way and shouted, "Hey, you!" He banged through the glass doors and out into the cold autumn air. He stumbled to the car and fell over the hood, panting, gasping for breath. He had never been so terrified, never so horribly frightened. It was as though someone had come up from the grave to whisper at him with decayed eyes. For one awful moment he had seen himself lying next to Emily, holding her in that somber, sullen coffin with the silver handles. It was ugly, it was terrible. He thought he was going to be sick. He turned his face aside, resting it on the cold metal. Then he began to sob; his whole body sobbed. Like a weak and hounded animal, he shook from head to foot and clung to the hood of the car. He was dying. He was a dying man. He was actually and terribly dying and being thrown aside. Like a funnel, the mouth of the ancient man in the white bed opened wider and wider and he saw himself falling, falling down that dark hole into endless oblivion, without hope, without joy, without honor or dignity, without even despair, falling into absolute and total extinction.

Then Margaret was beside him, standing there dumbfounded, her hands in her coat pockets. He raised himself slowly and looked at her. Her face was confused and pained and helpless and as far away from him as a face in a newspaper.

"I'll take you home," she said hoarsely. She opened the car door and he got in.

Later, after she was gone, he sat alone in the stuffed chair he had always sat in. His overcoat was still on and his hat rested in his lap. Everything was quiet in the house. The clock ticked gently over the mantel. Everything was familiar and certain and calm. The autumn afternoon crept evenly through the house, softening the edges, rounding the corners. He sat quietly and carefully, and gradually the life came back into him and he began to feel warm and comfortable.

Then he began to cry. It was quiet and easy crying. The tears fell down his cheeks, leaving shiny little lines. He knew he had reached the final thing, the true thing, and it was all right, and he was crying because he understood that it was necessary and all right. He sat for a while crying softly, and the room changed color with the falling sun and turned orange.

It was that time in the afternoon when he always took his walk. He rose slowly, tightened the muffler about his neck, put on his hat and went outside.

The wind blew crisply from the north as he walked the two blocks to the park. He went to his favorite bench and sat down. High above him the wind bent the tops of the trees and very high the white clouds rolled upon a blue sky. The leaves were falling and turning everywhere.

So, he thought, it just kept happening to you, life just kept happening to you. Even when you sat alone in your living room, events transpired. The sun came through the window and colored the furniture, the wind blew the curtains, the shadows moved upon the walls. You had to get up, had to dress, had to eat and move about and blink your eyes and feel the weight of your body on the soles of your feet, you had to undress and go to bed. In the great emptiness of nothing to do there was always something happening, some little life going on to hold you fast and make you guilty and afraid. And he knew it had been like that always, except that when he was younger and there was Emily and Margaret and the office and all his friends, the events were vast and complicated. They filled whole days or weeks or even years, intricate and twining around and within each other in huge webs of passion and thought and immense activity, so that he only came across himself in the mirror, like a stranger on the street. But it was the same. The events were only simpler now. A cough, the sound of a car going by out front, the rising and falling of his chest as he breathed, the leaves blowing across the wet grass on an autumn day. And as long as they happened, no matter how small, you paid attention and were misdirected from the truth, the only thing you could really get your teeth into, that you were alone, absolutely, totally and finally alone and that was the only thing you had to make peace with. He sighed and looked up.

She wouldn't get him in the nursing home, he thought, she would never try to tell him what to do again. Maybe it would even be a long time before she would come to visit him, because she was afraid of him now. He shook his head. It would be nice to begin life again. Well, then, many things would be nice to begin again. Men choose not to heed a dying man, and it's a wondrous deed, he thought, a wondrous deed. It's a marvelous thing, a mountain of a thing, a world of a thing. He sat alone in the park. The wind turned the edges of his hair. All around him the leaves were falling, falling and gathering softly upon the green and quiet grass.

Death Valley

It was all over now. He had loved her too hard and too long. They had spent too much time together and become too close so that when they were apart they grew a little frightened and thought somebody was to blame but it was only the two of them, wanting to be together and nothing else and then being afraid not to be.

Such things do not end easily and he didn't know what to do without her so he called her several times on the phone and asked her should they see each other again and maybe go to the park and drink frozen daiquiris out of styrofoam cups like the old days but she said that wouldn't be good and of course she was right and he knew she would say no but he called her two more times to ask again and hear her say no again and then, that last time, she cried and he knew it was dead, he was only punishing himself and her too. It's hard to let something you love die when it's still alive in an apartment on the north side of town.

So he decided to drive to Death Valley. He had only been there once as a kid and could remember nothing about it but it wasn't for the Valley so much that he was going but for all the distance in between and then not so much for that but for all the strangeness and the difference and finally the solitude, like a man who decides to sail all by himself across the sea to find out if he can.

He left the first day of Easter vacation and took the freeway to Reno to pick up 395. It had been another mild winter and already in late March the snow pack was melting off the Sierras and the farmers in the San Joaquin were worrying about the drought again but it was fine because the passes were clear and he wouldn't need the chains.

There was snow south of Carson City and then he found the little stream that runs beside the road. There was snow along the road and along the banks of the stream and he pulled into a deserted campground and climbed out of the car. He got on his knees and drank some of the water and then made snowballs and threw them into the stream. They rolled and grew wet and moved on down over the rocks, dissolving slowly and shining in the sun. Then he leaned against the car and smoked his pipe and watched the wind blow the tops of the pine trees. After awhile he got back into the car.

He made Bishop by dark because he wanted to be up early and into Death Valley in the morning. He found one of those older motels that are off the main street. It had no credit card shingles hanging from the sign and no neon lights. It was white stucco and a middle-aged woman had him fill out the register. The office was the front part of her living quarters and he looked over her head into the small room to where the color t.v. was going and a glass pot of coffee steaming on a two-burner hotplate. There was a stuffed chair with white crocheted doilies. A white cat was asleep on the lumpy cushion. There were mirrors on the wall and pictures of old people and a window with filigree curtains that opened to the street. When the woman took his money he saw that there was no ring on her left hand.

He drove the car around to the side and found the door with the number she had given him. There was a group of doors all in a row with numbers and only one other car parked between the white lines. He took out the suitcase and went into the room.

There was just the one room with a double bed and a small alcove with the shower and toilet. On either side of the bed were cheap laminated night stands with matching lamps.

Against the opposite wall was a vanity and mirror that was made like the night stands. Two inexpensive chairs with vinyl cushions stood just to the right inside the door. The walls were empty but there was a small color television chained to the floor on the far side of the bed.

He put the suitcase on the bed and washed his face with one of those little bars of soap wrapped in white paper. The towel was thin and white. Every motel he had ever been in bought the soap and the towels from the same place. Then he went outside and walked the two blocks to the main street to find a restaurant.

There was a steak house, one of those places where you choose a salad and drink and the waitress gives you a scrap of paper with a number and the kid with the funny hat fries your steak and then calls your number when it's done and you go up and it's waiting on the stainless steel counter above the grill where he's cooking and he says, "Thank you, sir, enjoy your dinner."

So he sat alone in a booth by the window and ate the cheap food and watched the traffic go by on the street. He was alone in the town and the night was coming on and there were the mountains across the way, purple and black above the buildings. The town was getting quiet and he knew that with the dark it would all be quiet, like small towns everywhere, and he was alone everywhere for hundreds of miles.

Then he thought about her and what she would be doing now and what she had always done at this time when they had been together, but that made him sad and he forced his mind to concentrate and he looked at the street and the cars going by and the colors of the buildings and the words written on the buildings and then up at the mountains, disappearing into the night. Then he walked back to the motel.

He opened the door and switched on the light. The suitcase lay like a familiar thing in a back room of lost and found objects. He opened it, took out his pajamas and shaving things and placed the suitcase on the floor. He put on the pajamas, brushed his teeth and got into bed.

He was all by himself in the bed and he had thought that

would bother him but it didn't. He liked the bed. He liked himself in the bed. He watched the wall where the door was. He listened to the different sounds and the quiet spaces in between. He liked being in the bed by himself with all the strange and different things. He was looking forward to the morning and he was tired from the day and wanted very much to sleep. He knew this time he would truly sleep. He closed his eyes and started to sleep. After a time the wind came down from the mountains and played with the phosphorescent edge of light at the bottom of the door. But he was sleeping.

In the morning he did not lie in bed thinking but got up immediately, shaved and dressed. He put the things into the suitcase and took the suitcase to the car. He drove the car to the restaurant and had breakfast.

He was on the road by nine o'clock and heading for the turnoff to Death Valley. The morning was very clean and clear and the light was wet and shining on the grass and on the leaves of the trees. Then he reached Lone Pine and made the turn east.

The road rose and fell, a grey, flat band pasted on the hills. Off to the right the wind raised the tall, curved towers of dust and dirt. The towers were as though of gauze and blew together at the top to form a trembling fan of powder and air that hung against the cloudless sky. The road dipped and climbed and moved in a long, turning arc toward the dry, open fields on which these towers moved in soft, slow-motion curls. He wondered if he would have to drive through them and what would happen to the car if he did.

But after a time the road turned away and he looked back at the towers finally and they appeared now to be dun-colored columns of thin smoke, all blown together like a veil or curtain. He had never seen anything like them. They must happen, he thought, because of the wind off the mountains. It was how the desert began.

And it was all desert. As soon as he had moved away from the eastern slope of the Sierras, it had been desert and now, with the dust funnels gone, there were only the rolling sand hills, the scrub brush and the lumpy, treeless mountains, hunched above the earth like the carcasses of gigantic beasts. He took out the thermos he had had filled at the restaurant and poured a cup of coffee into the plastic mug.

Then the sun moved higher in the sky but the air stayed cool and he kept the window down and watched the landscape roll by. There were not many people on the road and he was glad because the feeling was better that way.

After a time the road commenced to climb. It moved into the lumpy hills, cutting a rolling edge out of the sand and rock, and then levelled off to a kind of plateau. He rounded a curve and saw it.

At first he thought it must be Death Valley, but it was too soon. It simply appeared there, very far away and very wide, a deep, flat plain at the base of all the mountains. The road went to it and then across it in a straight line and then up into the mountains again. Death Valley, he surmised, was on the other side.

But this valley, whose name he did not know, was more beautiful than a sunset. It lay, empty and alone, at the bottom of the purple and brown mountains. The mountains were wrinkled and woven down to it and then there was this simple flatness, far away, all melted and still and even and hard. He pulled the car to the side of the road and stared at it. It was miles and miles away and yet he thought he might walk there in a few minutes.

It took him a half hour. The road turned and fell and the valley appeared and then was hidden by the slope of a hill. It was larger than he realized and when he finally got to it, the road went like an arrow straight across the floor and up on the other side. It must be part of Death Valley, he thought, like a calm bay hidden from the sea, a huge backwash of sand and stone.

Then he was across and he watched the valley in the rear view mirror. It dropped away as the earth does when you leave it in a small, single-engine plane and you look out the back window past the tail assembly. It had that same two-dimensional quality.

The road moved through the dry mountains and then he began to feel it. It was in the hills and the air. The sky became white-blue. The earth, which for dozens of miles had been empty and dry, seemed gradually to turn underside up, like a magnificent stone, to reveal the broken shards of unlived life. He realized he had not seen anything green for a long time and even the cactus, sprouting here and there, had a pale, sterile color against the dirt and rock. He became aware of an absolute and final solitude that seemed to burn from the earth and fill the air with a transparent, shimmering film. It reached into the car where he rode alone.

It offered absolutely nothing, only itself, iron and empty, and he knew that if he went out to it, if he tried to meet it on its terms, it would destroy him. Only by an act of imagination, an effort of creative will could he move out to it and let it be itself. That was the only way you could possibly live with it, he thought. And suddenly the car came over the final hill and he saw the mountains drop away and the sky and land become one, a kind of grey-blue unity, and for a second he believed he might fall off the edge of the world. The bones in his body were like the marrow in these hills. On the edge of nothingness his spirit rode, like a soul seated on a star rushing through space, and there was only one rhythm and one thing and it was beautiful, it was the most beautiful thing he'd ever seen, and then the car went over the hill and began going down, down to the Valley, always down, turning down, everything getting dryer and dryer and the sand and heat getting more and going ever down to the lowest, deepest hole in the earth, and he began to smile because he knew he had been wrong, it had just taken a long time to understand that nothing you truly love ever dies.

About the Author

Richard Dokey was born and raised in the San Joaquin Valley of California. He majored in journalism at the University of California in Berkeley. He now teaches and resides in the country, outside of Lodi, California. His fiction has appeared in leading literary magazines throughout the country and has been cited as "Distinctive" on many occasions in *Best American Short Stories*. Recently, Dokey has begun to work as a playwright. His most recent play is called *Craps*. He is also the author of a novel, *Two Beer Sun*.

About the Illustrator

Inara Cedrins is a printmaker who is working in the rare medium of wood engraving, a process in which a picture is engraved into a block of wood one line at a time. Her prints, and her writing and translations from the Latvian, have appeared in literary magazines around the country.

P. O. Box 10040
Chicago, Ill. 60610

Story Press is a small, non-profit publishing company committed primarily to the short story. We publish the Illinois Writers Series, called "a series to watch" by *Publishers Weekly*, as well as books by authors outside of our home state. Our hope is to bring recognition to writers working in a genre increasingly neglected by the commercial houses. Our previous books have won literary awards and we think our efforts are appreciated by the reading public. This book has been produced entirely without public funding, so your support is crucial.